THE ORIGIN OF THE FUTURE

ESSENTIAL TRANSLATIONS SERIES 59

Canada

Guernica Editions Inc. acknowledges the support of the Canada Council for the Arts and the Ontario Arts Council. The Ontario Arts Council is an agency of the Government of Ontario. We acknowledge the financial support of the Government of Canada through the National Translation Program for Book Publishing, an initiative of the *Roadmap for Canada's Official Languages 2013-2018: Education, Immigration, Communities*, for our translation activities. We acknowledge the financial support of the Government of Canada. *Nous reconnaissons l'appui financier du gouvernement du Canada.*

FRANCIS CATALANO

THE ORIGIN OF THE FUTURE

Translated by Jonathan Kaplansky

GUERNICA EDITIONS

TORONTO—CHICAGO—BUFFALO—LANCASTER (U.K.)

2025

Original title: *L'origine du futur*

Guernica Founder: Antonio D'Alfonso

Michael Mirolla, editor
Cover and interior design: Errol F. Richardson

Guernica Editions Inc.
1241 Marble Rock Rd., Gananoque (ON), Canada K7G 2V4
2250 Military Road, Tonawanda, N.Y. 14150-6000 U.S.A.
www.guernicaeditions.com

Distributors:
Independent Publishers Group (IPG)
600 North Pulaski Road, Chicago IL 60624
University of Toronto Press Distribution (UTP)
5201 Dufferin Street, Toronto (ON), Canada M3H 5T8

First edition.
Printed in Canada.

Legal Deposit—Third Quarter
Library of Congress Catalog Card Number: 2024945674
Library and Archives Canada Cataloguing in Publication
Title: The origin of the future / Francis Catalano ; translated by Jonathan Kaplansky.
Other titles: Origine du futur. English
Names: Catalano, Francis, 1961- author. | Kaplansky, Jonathan, 1960- translator.
Series: Essential translations series ; 59.
Description: Series statement: Essential translations series ; 59 | Translation of: L'origine du futur. | In English, translated from the French.
Identifiers: Canadiana (print) 20240454952 | Canadiana (ebook) 20240457196 | ISBN 9781771839495 (softcover) | ISBN 9781771839501 (EPUB)
Subjects: LCGFT: Literature.
Classification: LCC PS8555.A795 O7513 2025 | DDC C848/.54—dc23

To the Abenaki origins
of my grandmother Geneviève Messier,
whom I didn't know, but who nicknamed me
her Ti-Pouce.

But we are merely
once upon a time.
—**Leonard Cohen**, *Beautiful Losers*

Contents

FIRST MOVEMENT: LAND

The Plains

THE DAYS FOLLOWING a new moon, anything can happen. Even this excremental black night. It's mid-September and the weather is surprisingly mild. Dead silence reigns despite the night-time movement of the troops. It is the calm before the moment of truth. The ear only manages to detect whispering and the lapping of the waves, barely audible, caused by the flat-bottomed boats nevertheless filled with soldiers of the infantry. Every single one of them crosses the black waves toward l'Anse au Foulon, on the other side of the river.

The General's plan seems to be working well. One wonders if he didn't choose this night precisely because it is this night, or if his choice was mere chance. In any war, chance plays a role on the possible outcome of a battle, it cannot be stressed enough, it's even truer for the one being planned on the sly under cover of darkness, thanks to this incredible diversion over by Beauport.

Three flagships of the Royal Navy cover the amphibious operation. The landing, under the supervision of Captain James Shads of the Vesuvius, is done in dribs and drabs. The contingent of drummers, of which I am a part, boarded at the Point Lévy encampment. Another, which boarded at the western tip of Île d'Orléans, joined us aboard many barges and launches. The day of decision has arrived. It's make or break. The General is playing for high stakes. Among the eight cards he had up his sleeve, l'Anse au Foulon was his last and the most risky.

Can we speak of strategy here? Or of instinct? Of the instinct of a killer, or a gambler? Or is this the execution of a bizarre plan given that, often during the siege, the general had to contend with bouts of fever? These rogues of the French and Indian War, may they all drop dead. We will show them no pity. This war is very emotional.

In the boat carrying me toward the north shore, I am nervous. It's natural. I too am playing for high stakes. My tomorrows are indebted to this confrontation. Depending on whether we win or lose, I'll return to Great Britain, or perhaps to Germany to my county of Shaumburg-Lippe, or, who knows, I'll settle here with the money from my pay to begin a new life in this ex-New-France. Perhaps I'll also die, quite simply, honour where honour is due, on the battlefield.

In our camp, they say that the French general is particularly nervous these days. Although he has reinforced the lines of defence over by Beauport, he senses an incursion by the enemy upstream from Quebec. Yesterday again, he conveyed his anxiety to the Governor General of the colony, the Marquis de Vaudreuil, a man of whom he is not exactly fond. The latter replied to him: "We mustn't believe that the English have wings. We'll see about that tomorrow." Too late. Tomorrow is today.

> *I think Wolfe will act like a player of tope*
> *et tinque, who, after having played to the left*
> *of the tope, plays to the right, and then to the middle.*
> —Lieutenant General Montcalm

The path to l'Anse au Foulon is rather steep and very narrow. Only two soldiers can pass side by side, if they want to scale the cliff. The climb began at twenty past midnight, I know, I glanced at my fob watch. Four thousand and four hundred and fifty men, let's figure it out. Wolfe's six battalions drift down these narrows, sand through an hourglass, but upside down, from bottom to top, without anyone thinking to turn the accessory around. The Scottish highlanders are on the front line. With my snare drum fastened behind my back, I climb the path behind the drum-major, put up with it as best I can, clinging to the bushes and the shrubs to move forward, planting my boots in the fragments of shale.

Seen from afar, in the darkness, we must look like a colony of spiders weaving the web of a mad undertaking, fastened to our silken abdominal threads, heaving up toward the sky. We are at the back of the platoon, it must be four-thirty in the morning. We hear the last boats below scrape the gravel. We begin to hear the trill of birds. Red-winged blackbirds. White-throated sparrows. American robins. Almost no resistance from the French. Like a knife through butter. Clearly, they were not expecting us here.

At dawn, all the battalions were settled on the Heights of Abraham, ready to begin combat when the time came. As anticipated in the General's battle plan, I place myself on the right wing, close to the Louisburg Grenadiers led by Lieutenant-Colonel Alexander Murray. I await orders from the drum major to convey them to the infantry from the tips of my drumsticks. I await to be able to stimulate the troops, to be able to make them lose their heads with my drum rolls and my codified language.

▲▲▲

Outside Les Foufounes Électriques as on the flyers, no possible confusion: on September 13 at 8 p.m., the Irish band Stiff Little Fingers will headline, and in the first part, mine, The Nils, from Montreal, with whom I play the drums, and the other, Californian, Guttermouth. A crazy punk rock evening in store. High expectations. It's going to be electric.

Patiently I wind tape around the shafts of my drumsticks. It's my ritual. Before each show, I indulge in this meticulous, repetitive act that borders on the obsessive. Protecting my sticks from sweat. Make them easier to grip. If one were to slip from my hand during our performance, no one would see a drop. I'd keep the tempo, I'd get a reserve drumstick lying in the box by my side. Keeping control of the situation, not stopping playing, I'd roll another stick at the tips of my fingers, sure to not let it slip. Bobblehead spectators would be unaware of it.

The crowd is already dense in front of Les Foufounes, this bar and concert venue that regulars affectionately call "Hydro's backyard." I do some relaxation exercises, wearing my headphones: thumbs, forearms, shoulders. A few stretches to relax my sciatica, a few basic paradiddles performed on a sofa in the dressing room. I glance at the order of titles, traced in felt-tip pen on a bit of paper, knowing well that this order has no meaning, that it can be upended at any moment during the concert.

I'm ready to face the music. I always played by ear and that has served me well. I wasn't yet seven and was practising scales of *Smoke on the Water* on an electronic keyboard. By ear. And it worked. People couldn't get over it. Well. The rumour spread. Guttermouth jumps on stage.

▲▲▲

From here, the view is unobstructed. At dawn, it's magnificent to overlook our navy and watch it sail under the British flag at all the strategic points of the majestic river. The fortified settlement of the city stands on a powerful rock, as is already known. It resembles the bow of a ship. Due to its location, it stands like a natural fortress. The way a diamond can only be cut by another diamond, Quebec City alone could hope to carve Quebec City into pieces. It's protected by streams and cliffs along almost its entire length, on all its fronts, except one: the Plains of Abraham. As the regiments reach the top of the cliffs, Wolfe places them on the battle lines, back to the river. He obviously fears an immediate attack from the French, but which will never come.

It is a quarter after eight. Anyone who can predict anything now would have to be very shrewd, but I'd swear on it that the confrontation won't be long in coming. On one side and the other, we are on edge. I and my group of drummers and buglers are placed on the right flank, behind the 35th infantry, a brigade called upon to face the French snipers and the Indians waiting in ambush in the bush, who try, by all means, especially by carrying "the little war," to reverse the trend.

I am exposed to heavy firing from the militia hidden in the wooded areas, but that is the lot of any drummer to go straight to death, or else to give it rhythm, to put things in order, in a perfect mixture of discipline, heartbeats and patriotism. "Death will come and will have your eyes," the poet of Piedmont, Cesare Pavese, wrote one day. No, I am the cannon fodder type.

This morning, by the Foulon road, the sailors transported two light six-pound copper cannons, the only two, it appears, that our royal artillery will use, however, with formidable efficiency. The two armies, scarlet and white, one facing the other, are separated only by four hundred metres. It is almost ten o'clock when Montcalm, in a decision that is very bold to say the least, orders his troops to begin marching. The enormous flags flap in the wind. The drums rally the troops. My drum with its copper barrel pressing against my hip, I march in quick time, that is one per step second, sixty per minute, in normal time, as prescribed in *L'instruction pour les tambours* by the Comte de Bombelles printed a few years earlier, in 1754 to be more specific.

But I cut this rhythm short on the plains, as the first line of the French army, ranged in the centre in columns, has made up its mind to charge on ours, in a disorderly way it must be admitted. Lying on our stomachs to avoid the firing from the wooded areas to the side, our infantry line received the order not to fire a single shot before the enemy is less than thirty-six metres from the tips of our bayonets. It awaits the signal from our drums to comply. The French, on their side, in a rush to fight, have begun shooting at about one hundred and twenty metres. They don't know that on Wolfe's instructions, each of the muskets of our troops was loaded with two bullets instead of one, in anticipation of a heavy volley of shots.

The French line approaches, the left is already too far to the back and the centre too far to the front. The formation falls apart. Montcalm's error of judgment, of incorporating an inexperienced militia corps in each of the battalions, will prove fatal to him. We receive the order from the drummer corporal. With an abrupt roll on the tight skin of our snare drums, a sound that transcends the confusion and the smoke, we give the order for a salvo. At such a short distance, it is explosive. The infantry's Brown Bess muskets tear Montcalm's army to pieces. The confrontation didn't last more than a few minutes. The French are put to flight. The survivors flee toward the city, our troops on their heels.

▲▲▲

Singer Mark Adkins of Guttermouth is a great performer. His insolence is also legendary. His attitude aligns with the myth of spaced-out punk rocker, which he sustains quite well with his small spoon of powder hanging from his neck. Occasionally, a hyperactive or intoxicated spectator climbs on the stage, grabs the mic from the singer's hands, and sings in his place. The leader of the group is used to it, mocks his audience, dancing and gesticulating, doesn't give a damn about his performance, spits on people, shouts abuse at them. People like that.

Leaning toward his fans, crouching on the edge of the stage, through great confusion, to a distorted beat, the singer asks for the black leather jacket of the spectator who's closest, dancing in the orchestra. The jacket that he eyed before even the first note of the guitar was played. He wants to continue his show in this getup. He asks for the studded belt of another spectator who jumps in front of him. The guy obeys, unfastens the item from his waist and hands it to the singer, who tightens it around his wasp waist. In this new disguise, he wails into the microphone, sings, thrashes about, freed from something of which we're unaware, carried by the furious riffs of two guitars. The rhythmic section, a cannonade. In a style bringing together several musical genres, from skate punk crushed like a can of beer beneath a tire, to rapid rhythms pushed to their limits, to crazy, sarcastic, crazy punk.

Beer flows and you can smell it, everyone or almost is drunk, stoned or probably both, it's natural, you gotta let loose. It's September 13 in Montreal. An anniversary date, yes, indeed, two hundred and fifty years after — I found out later, much later — that harrowing battle on the land of Abraham *dit* "l'Écossais" (the Scot) and which was fatal to the French. This detail, this synchrony, I would say, this classic coincidence was revealed to me in a way by chance, good old chance and thanks to a good old dose of luck, two things of which all wars are made, and that decide their outcome.

The same old moon that in 1759, in its last quarter, illuminated — if you can call that illuminated — rue Sainte-Catherine, in any case it is no brighter than the amber Q of the Hydro-Québec sign that we see out of the corner of our eye from the sidewalk where many of us are out smoking a cigarette, chatting, taking advantage of deep breaths of air on this memorable evening while, on top of all that, we return to the stage after an absence of many years. Soon I will set up behind my drums, when the dust settles, the dust of Guttermouth.

As is the unwritten rule among drummers, I have brought my cymbals, my snare drum and my bass drum pedal. I can't give them up. These are extensions of my extremities. I adjust the height of my stool, another way of saying that I adjust my aim, and place my cymbals so that my gestures flow as required, have the force of impact sought and bring good news to people who need them and who, for this very reason, have come to see us throw ourselves into it for them, we who see them throw themselves into it before us. It's very, very quick. The Battle of the Plains of Abraham that drove the French from North America did not last longer than *Daylight, In Betweens, River of Sadness* and two or three other pieces played live. Fifteen minutes? Perhaps twenty?

▲▲▲

After Montreal's lethargic capitulation twelve months later — when I didn't have the opportunity to even touch an ounce of my gear — free finally, itinerant soldier, I was beginning already to fall in love with the Canadian land, a feeling that wasn't so different from the one the Weser Valley evoked in me. I began to become enamoured of the good brown earth of Quebec, of its river and its quiet strength, its romantic tributaries. I wandered from one village to another in the defeated New France, making a tour of I don't know what, unless it was myself.

To live, I buy trifles with the money from my pay and sell them on the way, a way that is often called the Chemin du Roy, me the pedlar with no fixed address, the traveling second hand goods dealer, or else I occasionally repair a fob watch or a pendant watch, clocks large and small, a stopwatch if necessary. Repairing the clockwork movement of these is my hobby. I like giving time life again. I set the order of the world to rights, size it up, like on the plains with my snare drum resting on my hip. And as they will one day perhaps do, who knows, some descendants from my line, including that one, Adrien, in the heat of the action in a smoke-filled bar in Montreal, tapping fills on his tom-toms, rasping his sticks on his cymbals and above all his super fast double kick drumming, imitating the military rhythm during combat, without his knowing, our troops made to toe the line, the enemy that must be put to rout, and this image of the frantic retreat of the French last fall at Butte à Neveu, which plays over and over again.

Then, just like that, I meet the love of my life, a Canadian. Françoise Fuseau, known as Roc, daughter of Mathurin Fuseau and Françoise Serre, born in La Visitation-de-l'Île-Dupas. This woman, larger and more beautiful than life, and what's more, with a head for business. Françoise gave me eight children, six sons and two girls, including twins who died at birth, in 1770.

We opened a drinking establishment on the Chemin du Roy in Lavaltrie, the Cross Pistols. It's our bread and butter. Business is going well. Our permits and certificates of good conduct are issued each year in due form. With our rum distilled in London, we have won over many customers, most of them merchants and travellers, others soldiers, mercenaries, loyalists but not only, also republicans, come to take sustenance at the Cross Pistols.

Amid this constant coming and going, impossible for the walls not to have ears. So, from little prince to drummer, from drummer to pedlar, from pedlar to clockmaker, from clockmaker to innkeeper, my life is made up of a long series of shifts. And perhaps, among the many hats I have worn, the one of informer should be added.

Laurentia

Stretching of the continent, from its uncompromising concavity. Ancient and new seas appear, better supported, glaciers, farther out than the other bodies of water. Because we are there, do the necessary passages, whether of ice or peat, lead to the north or to the west? The heart of meteorites beats in the embossing of craters. Distinct from its destiny, the soul of iron still today seeks a viable outcome for its interstellar voyage. Would it have been better for it to unite with more modern metals, such as nickel, or for it to strike the earth's crust in one go? The mid-Atlantic rifts henceforth pay no attention to these repercussions. It is too late. The moon trembles with its halo, shaken by pierced memories. An unimaginable quantity of fossils, found on the so-called rotating plates of the Earth, turn out to be stillborn. At this second, in the sea as in the atmosphere, a school of stoic coelacanths passes in slow motion. Fat snow flakes fall over Laurentia. From their unfathomable depth the oceans ascend the steep slope of elementary particles and yet no nautical chart mentioned this. This wind coolly polishes, smooths the edges of the emerged part of the icebergs, but it's still okay. And are the few scattered indications of humpback whales, of narwhals, sealions strewn on the bare valley? Does the blizzard crease our faces that plunge into the storm? Will it erase them? Laurentia slides towards its own shelf, loving and magnetic.

I will make appear
What is beneath the earth
Even if I must expose it to light.
—Chippewa poem

Large hourglasses without sand, form without substance, fragile, two ovoid translucent forms, thousands strewn on the ground. And this is Laurentia, a ready-made without a before or after, set down there, there, there and there, just about anywhere, in any case vertically on a vague territory, vast, excessive. Moreover, when it snows you'd think you were seeing one of those snow globes picked up in a souvenir shop, or a flea market, which, when shaken simulate a colossal snowstorm. We are what we are, you see, for we are still standing, nothing more. Does anyone have an idea of how little we have to do with the motor functions of a sphere? It's known, Laurentia dates from before the age of the daguerreotype, it's a flat surface where we go, close-up of our shoulders hunched over by things that don't yet carry a name, it goes without saying. We are dazzled by a flash of magnesium. The ice reflects many suns. Where does this desire to advance come from? What pushes us to carry on the work begun before by others? Would it be the slow journeys, perhaps against the wind? Would it be, from one erosion to the next, those spirits that dangle quietly above our true limits, our auras, hanging on them like on quarters of the moon? It is alas the bones of mammals lying on the ground throughout the way.

▲▲▲

Blowing snow or not, we head into the wind. Our walking is necessary but not indispensable. We are this herd of hominids progressing under the wide of eyes of language and the language is our sheepdog.

> Like the words that are placed in it, language finds us where we are. It picks up our confusion, indicates the star twinkling at the end of our index finger,

extended. Am I the one who will walk the fringe of the world a long time, will I lead the inhabitants of these ruins beyond peak winds? Am I even on the right side of the telescope or are we the image of an image of an image that treads on a glacier? Will I face white indefinitely, the burning look of albedo, me the trickster with his bergamask faces, carting around words in the air and down-to-earth gestures?

Laurentia carries along the faulted secret of its interior plates, unresolved. It is a conveyor that conceals, an uneven crust. A field more than terrestrial shakes the underlying burning chimneys. Are these supposed moving forests of conifers plausible? Perhaps at the surface, one world conveys another and the basalt and granite of a dream experienced in depth manage to move us like here, in fits and starts? Archaic earth floors overlap one another every which way and that is just fine speaking of stone.

Intercontinental memory turned toward the iron of the Far North. Floating memory that breathes, real ice cap set on the water like a cover on a pot. In the image of a long path outlined on the Earth, this extended memory never drifts, it unfolds, opens out. The Laurentian path moves so that it is shaken here and there, in the past as in the future, in the present like at the end, by unstoppable uplifts of mountains. Fractal structure of memory that drifts in the rounded sum of all its colours.

Farther on, volcanoes hold back to immediately flare up again in a muted flash. An archaeopteryx, heart beating, takes advantage of passing time to survey, hedgehopping, the desert landscape. The pupil of the winged creature is dilated, the reflection of a meteorite, no mistake, crosses the sky in its eye. A memory traced so far ahead by the global and invisible. This is a world like this current one, as there exist millions of others.

▲▲▲

A bit of simple survival has just appeared and once again, pebbles skipping on the water, it would smash right into the reefs that guard protohistory. Sensors of distorted dreams, we got moving, in the purest expression of our aim, we peacefully went the wrong way. Getting to point B didn't get us too far, considering that we were coming from point A.

A minimum of asymmetrical objects, twigs gathered up with a bit of this iron from meteorites and bundles of sticks from wood thrown just like that on our shoulders, did we wander as much as that above seas and worlds? And when was that? Did it date from the age of an abstraction? Was it only in the air, this distraction, this reaction? Once, we uprooted fire in the ground in Manchuria, brandished it in the darkness, a flame reminiscent of Lascaux, and it was clear from then on that without that incandescence maintained, and without us who praised it, the ancient Siberian plains would never have been discovered.

This blind march in time prefigures India precrushed by geographies. China ground by philosophies. It announced some Klondike reduced to powder. Companies and as many nuggets of Eldorado to the power of seven.

With no apparent aim, appetites compelling us, we walked in large numbers, salmons returning to the source, incontinent, exhausted at the surface of magnificent distorting mirrors. And this ground that crackled beneath our feet, was it as we first suspected, precarious ice bridges imagined by neglectful gods? Arriving ahead of straits and oceans with magma viscosity, reaching the Aleutian boundaries glimpsed here and there, at most our horde temporarily stopped beneath the weight of our scaffolds of bones.

> Crouched on the edge of the abyss, I imagine for myself a reversible world where time comes to its end like a film playing backwards. We would see ©olombus, ©abot, ©ortés, ©artier, ©hamplain and, why not, ©atalano, copyright in hand, backpedaling, and the Aztecs perhaps discovering Europe, and *homo laurentientis* tracked down by immaculate beasts going backwards along a flowered Beringia. We would see trees fall beside their fruit, rain restore the dehydrated cumulus, from bottom to top, in torrents.

Sinanthropus women, *tempus fugit.* Little sisters of Siam with, on the lower back, the tattoo of a yellow mark. Transparent Inuit women indolently playing ringette like so many blissful virgins lying on an icefield, are you really wandering effectively in this divided Beringia? Numb from head to toe and left behind in your superfluous pelisses, women, girls, little girls so curled up against the wolves, I see that you still weaken occasionally. Is it reasonable to repeat in real time that one day like your men you'll provide the craniums so sought after by the paleontologists of tomorrow?

The moon, straightaway on high, secretly jealous of the juxtaposable sun, and lined with a fluorcscent disk, through its cataracts attempted to adjust the lens on our odyssey. Along the glimmering tongues of ice, we continued on the path, dazzled, as has been said, already, by a flash of global magnesium, headed for the arbitrary, long ebony-coloured manes trailing on the ground, prognathous curves, decrepit skin, numbed pudgy fingers, of our human race.

Prisoners of a kaleidoscope concealed in all the twirling snow crystals, the path revealed during a crisis of phosphenes. We and these lured deer, did we really distance ourselves from the centre with whiteness? Were we dreaming of meat around the bone? The hunt had many Arctic zigzags. Was our gaze perhaps disturbed by ophthalmic migraines? Perhaps we should have embraced the quick and salty wriggling of the horizon. But this quick and salty wriggling of the horizon, even with its half smile, all tears in the eye excluded, did it exist before? And was it to the west, east, north or south?

> The shadow of a member of the deer family entices me up till the constricting crackling of the ice. What else must I persist in lugging around on my back, what other bundles of twigs, to what must I still venture, the Northwest so well implanted beneath the fat of the pituitary gland? Walking for a long time, a really long time, exhausted, above seas and worlds. Striding across straits, atolls, capes, mountain ranges. I am chilled to the bone, a sieve for the cold. I breathe down the neck of man and the moon is an eye incrusted in nothing.

It was snowing gently on the continental plate as it had snowed during the entire polished stone age. This phenomenon observed this morning, is it a polished omen? Is saying it tempting some umpteenth weather forecast? Is it "réaliser le réel," following the nevertheless felicitous expression of a poet dear to the beat generation, even its founder in denial, Jack Kerouac? At stake is the survival of our bunch of hominids, beings without ties who one day will set foot in the aforementioned America. In any case, same desert, same amnesia. Did we like this place as much as all that? Between you and me, did the places really have other choices than to dwell in us?

> Furrowed faces drift here and there in the blowing snow. I walk face into the wind, I, speaker of Inuit-Aleut whose destiny is immobile. Hair! Dazzle me like flocks of quartz in contact with this temperate breeze! Move away from my face turned blue! A figurehead for a star with my satchel, I take my distance from the suborder of simians.

So many sounds to describe snow, but not even one to say who I am.

> In this zone of uncertainty, tear down, migrate, fall, nomad to the most secret nevus on the skin. Going forward, always forward, turning my tongue of ice, back to the gust of wind, I quicken my pace toward the Chukchi Sea where essential climates prevail.
>
> Dust in the eye without an iris of the moon, here's the white in which from now on I find myself.

▲▲▲

Recognizing that our contemporaries have been suddenly propelled to a place that doesn't exist to now manage to maintain the flame of life until the pole made our vast velvet shiver. Then, with in our heads a split image of the North, did we even swoop down on other places, new ones, stripped of verticality? Admit that the previous assertion is true, the subsequent one must be as well, no?

What unfolds at this moment took place thirty thousand years before your Renaissance, before, how to say without repeating ourselves, that it, from the Italy of Raphael, Leonardo, and Michelangelo, in rather affected manner, detected us.

Balancing on the edge of a horizontal void, it is highly possible that a simple flick of Man's DNA can lead us to this whirl of wandering. Is it possible, given that we are still turning? The idea of a highly boreal probability accelerated our entry into the spiral of time. Is not this entry, in the end, another way of saying our fall? And this fall, isn't it that of a wild animal? And isn't this wild animal the Great Bear and the Northern Star technically set ablaze?

It appears that right before us there opens a black abyss that itself opens onto a white abyss. Abysses in black and white. The pole of life, the pole of death, you have to decide, or it's better to drift between the two. As many cobalt blue skies asleep on the wrinkled, nickel-plated napes of our necks, in a famished assertion, we pushed on to the Ungava triangle and as the climate removed its shawls one by one, gently the ice, seen from the air, it's terrible, had a desire for water, and to return to it.

▲▲▲

Modeled on a moon powered with nitrogen snow, with loud groans the sun frees our small blue planet from its immense ice cap. An extremely slow phenomenon that requires that a god dreamed of us spontaneously, hyperborean. So many sleepless nights, so many dark afternoons, during which were we not also dreamed of by our manitou in the grass, an improbable outline walking alongside the bone of a reindeer cut up on the spot, cut off from the tribal council? And the song of the whales, those audio frequencies, micro-religious, was it no more or less in the perspective of accompanying our desire to go dogsledding?

> In simultaneous translation, and accompanied by false friends, we made worrisome discoveries. Like this one that by patting the mouth firmly with the palm there resurfaces at the backs of throats, at the very bottom, sounds deeper than a harpoon, less high-pitched than a fish hook.

Is it the desire of an unappeased cloud? Is that a flight of white geese directly emerging from a dreamlike game of dominoes? Is it I who will perform real spirals in a real sky? For want of being fooled, our jubilant children beat wings more than is needed and, preceded by wheezing cries of contentment, strongly resembled megamystic penguins.

> Forecasters of the word "snow," silent image that liquifies on contact with the tongue, we saw a shower of desires slowly falling from the skies, cuticles, red shavings, as it were.

It's quite obvious, it electrifies us to feel behind these shields of mist a river pouring out, turning in this way, and we will always be free to take it, downstream or upstream, with all our senses or without, in a terrible state. All along this limestone lung, time has an aspect of a four-legged creature where the seasons do better than sit up and beg, they display their colours fully. If the winter of frozen rivers, even lakes, chases us from the indissoluble source, summer, on the other hand, pursued by the tiny nibbling lips of spring, rekindles a feeble hope to live another season of Eden.

We are dealing with ferruginous memory, basalt, milky, granite, of man, tree, grass. Of river, stream, fish, goose. Would it be a memory of steel, this voice whispering to us all these words in the folds of the back of the neck?

> There is no river better connected to the universe that was created so small to throw itself in this way, on a large scale, into the ocean, nor a river more alone that takes its name from an incomparable anonymous fault. Is it indigo blood running in the veins of a canoe man breathing heavily? Isn't it instilled by the West? Doesn't he shrink there? And isn't the river, seen from here, from this cape widened by gusts of wind, rounded by these terse and rocky words, a habitat for krill? Didn't enigmatic whales in the Cretaceous period have all the time to dive down? The river is a sob shed long ago by the greatest of Saurians, the black sob of dinosaur today lying beneath the silt, in this deep embankment of clay.

From the source of the five lakes, the big river swells with great ceremony toward the estuary and no one was able to touch the bottom, as there is no bottom in its name. Is there a bottom to "St. Lawrence?" Are we still in Laurentia? That is the question.

SECOND MOVEMENT: ICE

Storms of the Century

I KNOW ALL ABOUT the repercussions of a storm. My son was born during the Gulf War, during the "Desert Storm" phase, and I, quite simply, I turned thirty the day the Iraqi Army sabotaged the oil installations in Kuwait, in the port of Mina-al-Ahmadi, setting fire to it, and creating an incredible oil slick in the Persian Gulf. I was born for monster storms. To mark my thirtieth birthday, we decided to spend the upcoming months in Ixtapa Zihuatanejo, Carolina F. and myself, of course bringing the baby. To complete the picture, the day before our departure, southern Quebec weathered a snowstorm. It was described as historic, without exaggeration.

The repercussions of a monster storm have something good: it is always dead calm afterwards. What they forecast indeed arrived, despite the risk of error, and the flurries, and the blizzard of the previous day, definitely real, are finally relegated to the status of a memory, still recent, but a memory. Montreal resembled a desert without cacti. The snow dunes and drifts gave the landscape a folded shape that called to mind sheets at the foot of a bed, pushed there by warm toes, after a torrid night. You could make out cars on the Plateau — and other neighbourhoods — worn out under enormous bell jars, that sooner or later, to get them out, would have to be cracked with our shovels in order to reach the interior, whose white shell would need to be broken to remove the body of the young bird, dead, killed in the egg.

Through the window I look at the magnitude of the task, the expanse of white. Albedo is having a wonderful time, illuminating everything and making it cold, whereas the speakers are spluttering *1990* by Jean Leloup — *c'est l'heure des communications*. It's time for CNN, in fact. A war of mediation, of awareness, of manipulation. War live, as reality TV, as a video game, GIs in the desert filming with their cell phones, basically rudimentary, images taken from life of an old conflict of fake news and relaying them to a scattering of hand-picked journalists. The famous surgical strikes. When it comes to manipulating public opinion, and not only that, the United States is still today difficult to beat. Past masters. Fortunately, our suitcases are ready. All that's left is to clear the snow off the Chevrolet Cavalier stuck in this desert of ice.

▲▲▲

It is through the door of January that I enter my thirtieth year and it is through this same accessory that we arrive in Mexico, wound up and in tune with the spirit of the day. The customs officers in the airport are quick to stamp the passports, they're not fooling around with the ball on a soccer field. Our baby is very well-behaved. He did cry a bit when the plane began its descent. He's a tough one. He didn't flinch one iota when they stuck a needle against tetanus and hepatitis in his arm. Nothing. Not a cry. Not even a tear. Future warrior. Defender of music. Drummer. Who performs behind the group, is its heartbeat, stimulates the troops, keeps the tempo, so that everything remains on track. Aside from a two-day bout of diarrhea treated in a Mexican clinic, due to the water from the pool that he swallowed, he caught nothing. It is in this hyper-protected condo complex in Ixtapa, where most of the owners are American, where at night you hear alligators frolicking in the stream next to a golf course, that Adrien the-little-Tabarnaco cut his first tooth. A foretaste of his first drumskins.

I walk along this dirt road between Ixtapa and the little village located further south. Sometimes, a bus sweeps by, windows broken or inexistent, a long rosary that sways hung on the rear-view mirror. A little bit back from the road there are makeshift houses, groups of huts of Roman *borgata* reminiscent of the neorealist wave of Italian film in the 1950s, favelas, like I would see in Lima, Santiago de Cuba and Valparaíso, all these lightbulbs fastened to a wire, all these sheet-metal constructions. I walk, it is my wish to be alone. I have reached the middle of my life journey, not so much the one in terms of physical age as the other one, which corresponds to an uninterrupted flow of natural and trivial events, and more or less random social choices — birth, studies, work, family — I have reached the first words of a comedy that deep down has nothing too divine or too amusing.

We are in Mexico and learn that my mother has suffered a heart attack at Promenades Saint-Bruno. Filippo took her to the hospital, to emergency. An operation that requires a double or triple bypass, they'll open her rib cage, where her little wounded heart is struggling. Grafting of arteries will follow, transfusions. She will recover, this resident from Ohio assures us, our neighbour in the condo, drink in hand, immersed up to her waist in water at the pool. This pool where an unusual alligator came to take a dip in the night of the nineteenth. After all these years, why does my father still say "allagator" and "coccodrile"? He cannot get it into his head. "In the ass yes, but not in the head," as the bawdy Roman proverb goes. She will recover, medicine is an established science. A surgical procedure like another. Must trust progress. Coming from the mouth of Madame from Columbus, why not? It's our only hope.

The cardiologist used language full of imagery: a heart attack, she maintained, and a snow storm, are the same thing. We had a gift for evading cardiac storms and heavy snowfalls. You need to have the South in your skin, a kind of compass, neurological GPS implanted in the left hemisphere of the brain — start, quit — or in the southern hemisphere of the planet when the imaginary is written. You just have to shovel while breathing through your nose and bending your knees to avoid a herniated disk, taking breaks, to prevent the arterial plaques from crystallizing in the arteries and sending us straight to the Heart Institute.

▲▲▲

We are driving in the starry night somewhere between the state of Guerrero and Ciudad de México. The sky reflects the billions of homes lit up on earth, so many houses stretching as far as the eye can see, lightbulbs suspended from a wire like us, myself, Carolina F., Adrien, clinging to the segment of our journey, erratic birds landed on erratic blocks. The bus drives by nocturnal mountains and deserts, the baby is sleeping soundly, the head of my sweetheart resting on my shoulder, we're wandering through the world, a small moving dot in North America seen from the sky followed by the eyes of Aztec gods.

No new world without a new language.
—Ingeborg Bachmann, *The Thirtieth Year*,
tr. Michael Bullock

The headlights illuminate the orange cat's eyes inserted along the highway asphalt, as if we were following a coloured line, an illuminated corridor, a virtual road, we are users of an inexistent bus and passengers in a video game where the player at the commands suddenly decides to stop off in Acapulco. Just in time to watch, in a dream, the spectacle of the diver, the man who launches himself from atop a cliff into the warm waters of the bay, an echo of the Tomb of the Etruscan Diver. Turning around, I see a Nahuatl girl brushing her long black hair and looking at herself in a compact disc. An “allagator” slides gently into the water of the pool. Written on a sign: “Don’t disturb the iguanas.” It is probably already mentioned in some proverb, but climbing stairs is good for the heart, that’s all the more true at Teotihuacan where I reach the top of the Pyramid of the Moon at the moment that Mexican fighter plane passes at low altitude, it’s enough to push someone into an apocalyptic roar, spinning with sacrifices, decapitated snowflake, heart ripped, they pushed me to the bottom of the scarlet hypotenuse. From all islands I return bare-chested, a T-shirt swapped for a joint of local pot, a polo shirt for a snorkel, to see a cornetfish, I’d play *Smoke on the Water* on a coral keyboard, eyes closed.

In the headphones, mainly *Wish You Were Here* and *Animals* prevail. I’m lying on my stomach facing the ferocious waves of the Pacific. The waves rise up and collapse. Children utter wheezing cries, defy the back-and-forth of the waters, deep down they’re deathly afraid. Tourists pulled by a speedboat, hanging on to the Icarian pleasure of a polychrome parachute and flying over the rows of swimmers and the rocky peak standing at the west of Ixtapa beach. Like everyone, I have nine orifices, and each makes a link between the inside of the body and the outside world. Music in the ears increases the acuity of the other senses, canals wide open, except for the anus and the opening of the urethra, in the bathing suit, sharpened on the old stone mill of the eternal present, on the ocean sandpaper. I found the jackpot! Lying in front of timelessness, rechargeable battery, didn’t André Breton say that Mexico is a surrealistic country? I let sand flow quietly through my fist. I am a horizontal hourglass lying down. An ice cube in a glass of whiskey. The drunken worm dead at the bottom of the bottle of tequila that you swallow with the last drop. That worm is my brother.

It Was Before

It was before the fall of Troy and the foundation of Rome. Before the Epic of Gilgamesh, the Song of Songs, the *Histories* of Herodotus, of Livy, the eruption of Vesuvius in 79 or the tsunami of Santorini, Pliny the Younger and *The Jesuit Relations* of New France. It was before the Egyptian scribes, the Rosetta Stone, the incunabula of *The Divine Comedy*. The medieval illuminations, the retranslations, copyist monks, newspaper sellers, whistle blowers, Court informants, moles, spies. The divulgers of myths, the cartographers of the soul.

It was before Homer's *Odyssey*, the Champlain Sea, the ice of Wisconsin, the Monteregian Hills, the Appalachians. It was before Giordano Bruno and the Inquisition, Galileo and his recantation, Amerigo's America, Magellan's circumnavigation, before Amsterdam, Antwerp, the republics of Genoa and Venice, John Cabot, Cleopatra or Hannibal waging war on the back of an elephant. It was before Mount Royal that has been trickling for ages as these lines are being written and before the island of Manhattan, the trading posts in Tadoussac, the shape of the Great Lakes, the Finger Lakes, the uplift of Mount Washington.

It was before the amazing about-turn of heliotropes, the resilience of ginkgo, the opening of *Galanthus nivalis*. When the most difficult part of our advance was yet to come, we watched in a dream wild horses grazing or herds of mustangs galloping in the mauve American pampas. But was the dust of dawn that arose above their hoofs gold nuggets?

muscular oaks dogs police horses oaks with large fruit
photographs and sunflowers Franciscan heads
oak-fruit white or bicoloured according to delirium or not
—Paul-Marie Lapointe, *Arbres*

It was before Mesopotamia, the Acropolis, Sana'a, Great Britain, before the Inca Trail crossing the Sacred Valley, the Apache Trail studded with cacti, the Grand Canyon over which an eagle circles and Persepolis and cuneiform writing. It was before the Caribbean Sea overrun by ships, before the vermin coming and going trundling along at the bottom of the holds of three-master ships of sweating conquistadors, parked in those coves giving off, alas, the stench of brine.

It was before smallpox, variable geometry influenza, the Spanish flu, COVID-19 and its variants, inflation in Europe, Rasmussen Peary & Co, before Alsatian sledges, Normans with amphi-biological longships and Basques returning from the cod banks. It was before the "totality of facts" (Wittgenstein). But was it before the Man of Similaun, the mummy of Ötzi, little Juanita sacrificed at the peak of the Andes? Was it before *homo faber* now busy over an artefact, his face reflected by the face of a flint? Before the Siberian plateau where we slid, peaceful, or before this inexplicable sled runner, abandoned like a relic on an icefield of this vast world, without beacons or other markers?

▲▲▲

A world compact and white, is it true, did we roll along in Beringia the whole time on a geometric shape, an isosceles trapezoid, pure, hard, stretched out, whose hinge in the shape of a horizon was plumbed with blue? Did we run behind the shadow of a morning very close to Mongolian, a real human mass on the move, a drawing of which the Sinanthropus ancestor would have been proud.

He would have watched us progress with an eye to producing an instant mosaic, us, pushed into the spiral of time, launched brusquely forward on these slippery tessera, gigantic, at the junction of space and vagueness, of the arbitrary and the concluded. Where are we coming from? Where are we going? Being the straw man of a star, its exhausted radiance, the pretext for cryopreservation. Will we walk eternally like this with fussy little steps?

Was it well before Magna Grecia that slips between our fingers, from north to south? Do the points of the compass melt? Certainly we have migrated, wandered, passed, hurtled down, drifted, extrapolated, fallen, we gathered together, insinuated ourselves, progressed, roared on the continent and for a long time, a very long time, forsaken in the clan. But beneath our steps isn't it possible that the glaciers were moved as well?

> *Oh! The banner of bloodied meat on the silk of seas and of arctic flowers: (they do not exist.)*
> —Arthur Rimbaud, "Barbarian," *Illuminations*, tr. A.S. Kline

A question of supporting our presumed geolocation, our welcoming women have rubbed our muscles with the warm blood of killer whales without jurisdiction, for the roads were interminable, our wives were accustomed to the northern lights and time did not exist. No intention, no finality led us here unless it was this alarmed deer, a fugitive of distances, antlers standing tall to the sky, eyes timidly dotting infinity, fleeing the dawn soaked up in a clearing. Did he want to lose us toward another expanse of Beringian ice?

Immediately, we entered into ourselves, set up a makeshift camp. "We," was it under cellophane? Sous vide? Kinds of *matryoshkas* fitting into each other ad infinitum only reaching, to our knowledge, just one season, just one life, would we succumb, for all that, each night, to listening to the Pleistocene moaning of whales? All the same, we followed the Northern Star at dusk, our primitive twilight viaticum.

In the daytime, beneath a sky that inflects the ice, we slide with the black spots that have since adorned the sun, but it's approximate, sixty-two million fuchsia moons. The Siamese dawns had left us when two boreal suns reflected their image back to us. Gradually, the dawns piled up behind us who, without even turning around, thumbed our crooked noses in the half-light of prehistory. Under the continuously skewed action of a trepan to form a flurry of wood shavings, then uncertain mounds of tin, we followed our Great Bear very carefully. In any case, we tracked down the traces of its urine, its odious odour, strong, bitter, vivid, that with a polar circle marks the whole territory where we then progressed circle by arctic circle.

Nomadic from head to foot, we are down to our most secret mole. We can't be more nomadic, can't be more migrant, can do absolutely nothing, it is almost certain we have made high spirits our spiritual antithesis. Forward! Always forward! When did we leave for the Aleutians, do you remember? Squat, plump and Asian, we seemed to be air deflectors, smooth, as if the blizzard with potential frostbite parked in our long black manes had shaped us.

> Forward, let's go! Always farther! But toward what South? Meeting which civilizations, because usually don't they take the opposite axis? When will we leave to hunt the Great Bear and polar bear?

The elders are found to the left, their speech strung with ice cubes. Faces veiled by the opaque smoke, roughed out by a philosopher's stone long exposed to the flagging passage of the wind. Veterans floating in ample sealskin underwear, reckless, of ice, mimic, not without technique, the element that they defy.

To the right are found children who evade matrilineality, what is conceptual in it. Young and old are the two immediate poles, we drift between them toward nowhere as we come from nowhere. The old, the children, would they be the obsessive leitmotiv of our expiry date? Why devote to them this unanalyzable cult?

▲▲▲

Would our well-honed soul as hunters become, just by thinking of it, a floury purée, a lumpy oatmeal simmering in the hollow of our hip bones? And us, during that time, progressing between knowledge and lack of knowledge in the heart of the icecap, in an uncertain language, armed with a minimum of archaic objects, and inventing little by little a rhythm to these hyperborean lands, with our multipurpose legs, appropriate. All the while endorsing the melody of a song still to invent, we went on this double isosceles trapezoid that lies upside down and does not end, in the direction where north meets south but no more than that. No more than that?

Two worlds with two different plans cutting into one another under the irisless eye of the moon. There is the world and its double. We are there. We're in between, in pure distance. Time passes, space expands.

While the Ancients held ad hoc councils, spontaneously, in the background, we dared debate magnetic fields, from the obligatory Northwest Passage to the Chukchi Peninsula, from the game hunt and constellations in the shape of a stunned seal. We waited silently for the oneiromancers with reindeer antlers on their heads to advise, they who, in a dream, had glimpsed the chosen land. And this land, was it at the bottom of a kaleidoscope, on the flatness of a puzzle made up of meadows and mounts, of atolls, of medicinal plants, ginseng, lilies to watch grow, corn as high as the moon, beans as far as the eye can see, polychrome fruit, an abundance of papayas and pumpkins, tomatoes and tubers, seeds expanding the glebe, or, in other little words, was the chosen land stuck to a mosaic buried at the bottom of a large lake?

A wild land to the north, covered in pines, thorns, brambles, raspberry bushes, groves and crossed by never-ending indigo fluids. A tropical land to the south, liana strewn with yuccas where rhesus monkeys coexist with hummingbirds, where the steppes abound with pumas and burrows of deceitful chinchillas, where Aataentsic rushes up, wise among the wise, an angel without wings who flies and blows like a white whale to announce the happy, messianic news to the group.

It promises nothing less than a land of plenty, then noon and midnight rise up unenergetically above harsh northern lights, there is the vision watching the setting sun of the yellow mark of Siam. This provokes a clamour of joy, a flight of frivolous spirits in a clan rigidly rising against the raging blizzard, a foretaste of the advent of the totem poles of the west, which augurs well.

▲▲▲

Are we just missing the reference, the right acoustic message to announce God? Aataentsic closes the gaps, fills this void with a voice off camera, with its harangues supported by structures of bones. Did Aataentsic die yesterday, dazzled by a final vision? This controlled hallucination robbed her of some pigments of life at the bottom of her mortar, pyrites, and perhaps even home fires.

Dawn had just risen when a faded rose, come as an image from we don't know where, immediately straightened up to salute it, and the horizon really snowed, it was a duvet, it was a wonder. Then the suns, long having undergone trephination, opened patches of electric blue sky, the sawdust flew, then the wind blowing from a steel lung activated its bunch of keys in the pure and dry air that drew us in just one block from an artificial coma. A cacophony of which we should have read the warning sign in the creaking of a heavy door opening onto the village of souls, a village itself opening onto heartbeats.

Our sobs stable on piles of bones, we carefully wrapped the remains of Aataentsic in fur that is half mink and half sable, but will the bears and white wolves carry away, and in them their metabolism, her quality of man without fault, his courage, his strength and his loyalty still tattooed on his skin, toward the final stage of the day? This death cast a terrible cold.

▲▲▲

The wind rose to moan again, the snow had twinkled on our faces, but at this stage we were fighting the cold with cold, homeopaths without energy and, like a debt toward the stupefying law of nature, with no more god, enveloped in simple flesh for any alleviation, we persevered on our way, alone among them, numerous in the shade and vice versa, the universe sawed in two.

Wandering, resilience, *Tekhne*. Our women continued to give birth on the surface of icy vermillion lakes that one day would carry their name. Is nothing less certain?

The idea of urgency attracts our blessed bodies straight ahead to the west, where the blue hinge is gradually oxidizing. The animal perceived ahead, with its unusual rump by way of a star, we wanted to inhale it to clay, wanted with our various tools that by their shape, by the matter with which they are made, become knife and assegai, we want to cut it up fairly like you tear a territory to pieces to offer it to the unfolding of seasons plated with alabaster. Aataentsic's skull, preserved below freezing, is it wise to make a gift of it to posterity?

▲▲▲

How much time must we still knock around on the uncompleted ground before thinking of returning to lands glimpsed at by our defunct god? This crackling beneath our feet that never tire of advancing through granular snow, this rumour that sticks close to us at all time, keeps the rhythm, the pace. If there is no smoke without fire, it's because we are advancing on embers of nitrogen.

> Icebergs crisscross the shores of the aforementioned Beaufort Sea, or was it before, they are in fact smoking, burning, and seals and sea lions on their upside-down hull lounge there, languid.

Would we pass along the Tropic of Cancer that actually would be the Sinai inverted, a transparent hourglass and snow globe mingled together. We pass along these imaginary lines without knowing, our unconsciousness rises to the surface of the water, climbs the white ruins of the day before, then slides to the abyss like whale soap. The points of harpoons in progression takes on the exact shape, though a bit rough, of our prey and sometimes heavy mammals, such as these woolly mammoths, fallen inanimate, or, like these sea-lions, rise again, slain, to the surface from top to bottom, or inversely but always by ending at the foot of our animal instinct.

▲▲▲

We thank the spirit, that of all things. It knows well the cycles and redundancies of feasts in such a way as to leave nothing to the hard-working hyenas, nor to the bears, those two-season half-gods, their stomachs weighed down. It becomes drunk from the auras of our bodies. Water no longer responds to the signals emitted by our thirst. Our tongues are rough. It is one of those feasts where we burst like flesh opening against a flint arrowhead, where for one night we are sated under the waxen moon. Is it an impression? It resembles a famished communion wafer shaded by a hoard of black clouds. Reaching the climax of an extraordinary tarantella, why would we hardly see ourselves capering about on the horizon, while we are there, cathedral frescoes in trompe-l'oeil and convoys of carts and wheels? A mass of men, women and children marching to the apex of the Great Bear, like for a stampede to the ordinary?

Nevertheless, we sensed the long turn ahead, a hyperbole inflecting the depths of time. All the mornings of the world removed their layers of skin one by one. Would Earth return to its bed? Did the climate suddenly become dizzy? Had it been dealt the blow of labyrinthitis? One thing is sure, we felt a stir above our mops of hair. The glaciers, without warning, slipped their white blouse off the coasts, and outcrops of territory detached themselves in a block from the continent, set off drafting, left to stretch out in the distance.

Destitute, we watched the scene, neither hot nor cold, the preview of a sequential deglaciation, yet a light breeze, arising from the astral gulfs, faraway protohistoric peninsulas, blew amorously on our round faces, relaxed, some sallow, others bronzed. From our foreheads a number of rare aquatic birds took flight, quartz flecks on a slack sea that wrinkled suddenly. If our hair sprays us at low tide, it's because of the sweet tender breeze of yesteryear.

▲▲▲

Will we continue to excessively waterproof our makeshift shoes? Will we clear off, transmigrate still for a long time? Our taste for adventure is carried by the idea of an igloo on wheels outlined in the distance, at the hinge of a double isosceles trapezoid. And the strengths drawn from the depths of our sisters sit crudely in the spirit of invention, in our walk that all in all is pragmatic.

> Walking and composing are one, that is the Aleutian formula for progress brought to its most simple expression, for whoever says stagnate says decompose. That is our motto.

Is it this idea that we depict when we say "shifting?"

> Perhaps outlines of landscapes are born in shifting, where pictures of whiteness burn. There we abandon the pictogram of our steps. By letting ourselves drop there, the snow interprets from below, gathers, calculates, adds up the packed-down air bubbles.

Is this dog who is sleeping still entitled to call himself a dog? And all of a sudden the group moves like a game of light sliding on an oil stain, or like two maple leaves very close, fallen simultaneously on the surface of a river, drifting off, and the distance between them grows exponentially where the current leads it.

These mutts that followed us and still do from the Siberian plains, that keep us company and that we have tamed, why, since we are dog-lovers, not harness them?

We travel through the lands of Ungava strewn with reindeer, seals, bears lapping all types of fluid, just like we hurtled down the hazy vision of a Laplander leaning over a source. The group began walking after one day having straddling the gears of Bering. We have always wanted bone and water, a stag capering by, a river hardly ever used over there. It's hot, is it so strange? We relieved ourselves of kilos of skins as the climate removed a weight from its shoulders and we were devils and were also dogs. Abundance reigns, fishing and hunting a pair, also going at a good pace, and in the opposite case, if a food shortage had begun to make us look unwell, would our dogs have changed anything?

> The raw flesh of dogs, harder than that of walrus or narwhal, does not rival in flavour with it. We possess several Samoyeds, yes, they belong to us, yes, they have eyes as piercing as icebreakers, white fur, immaculate to drive you mad. Why, once again, not harness them to these recently built sleighs?

Follow the assembly directions conveyed in a dream at the dawn of an impossible dream. Arrange! Tongue and groove! Chop! The assembly isn't that difficult. Whale ribs carved like skates support a structure of reindeer kept in place with the help of leather straps and hup, each family has a sleigh, each family its Volkswagen Bug, its piece of Ikea furniture, its team of utilitarian dogs, swift, diligent.

▲▲▲

It's important to know how to seize these flashes as they pass, that court Arctic intelligence and genius, know how to bend the whip. Also we made a pact with our dogs to forge concepts as vital as speed and traction. Was the conquest of this until-now virgin land within our reach? Did we slide so skilfully that we were called tightrope walkers on a wire covered in black ice, did we really slide to where the sun neither sets nor rises? Does something lead us to believe this? Does the memory of a face still drift here and there in the thick blowing snow?

Who is led to the gleaming west, who to the south straddling innumerable ice bridges, and who remained, but I with others continued gullibly to Ungava. Am I on the verge of thinking about a Winnebago? No doubt. And the group dispersed for better or for worse. It was implacable.

▲▲▲

Do these words — dog, continent, skates, dawn, iron, face, snowdrop — exist? Are they but a substance far removed, things on which we have no hold, traces melting like ice on a burning idea? The unattainable place of a desire to say? It is perhaps the primal cry of First Peoples scattered on this colossal territory, a great cry marked with visions, and nothing other in the absolute, nothing. A mimetic migration, the cathartic stammering of my people carried away by the wind, small skins surveying mountainous peaks and a very calm sea, like a billion stupefied monarch butterflies.

In this place somewhere close to an avalanche path, only a thousand feet from entering into the history without history of the Inuit-Aleut, we finally untied the dogs from the sleds. Something tells us that we had still not emerged from the Cross Pistols.

THIRD MOVEMENT: MEN

The Crossing

THE PORT OF NAPLES. 1953. The ferry terminal is teeming with people. Migrants mainly, accompanied by members of their family, but sailors as well, customs officers, port personnel, newspaper sellers. There are also people selling seafood by auction behind their stalls, whose lilting voices pass lightly above the agitated crowd, above this cacophonous back and forth. Angioino Quay, where an ocean liner has just berthed, is also jammed. You'd think you were at the beginning of an economic, demographic boom, but I wouldn't know how to say what part of the world will profit from this very real excitement and who it will make happy.

Mingling with the crowd, a man stands out, dressed in a suit and cap. It's my son. He is not yet thirty. In this outfit, he seems to have renounced his social condition. But that isn't the case. He is too proud. If he's leaving alone for America, it's to live life fully, to change, to experience adventure. He stands up straight on the quay, like a bouquet of bougainvillea. Almost all the family has come, my sweet wife Angela with our eldest, Mario, our grandson Giovanni, and also Carlo, a cousin, who has made the journey in his old Fiat 500 Topolino. They're all there, mingled with this original big bang, this jumble of people. Except me. I saw fit not to come. I preferred to rest in the fields and take care of the fruit trees, farmyard animals, keep myself away from teary scenes, from goodbyes, from break-ups, far from those devasting episodes where mothers press sons against their hearts, wailing unbearably.

The *Homérique* slowly detaches itself from the dock, slices through the waves in the Parthenopean Bay. The man on the deck resembles just about anyone, except for the crew on a merchant ship. He is sitting on his blue suitcase, for fear it will be stolen. He knows what Southerners are capable of. While it is humanly possible, he casts a last glance over the port. He sees Castel dell'Ovo and Palazzo Reale slip by, sees ferries heading for Capri or Ischia. Vesuvius in the background, the *sterminator Vesevo* that Leopardi speaks of in a poem, stands out in the twilight sky. Its presence is intimidating. It is frightening, but you become used to it. My son can no longer make out his family who grow smaller on the quay and who he leaves there, to their miniature destiny, to their black earth, blacker than ever. The handkerchiefs waving in the distance is actually a flock of seagulls.

▲▲▲

This young man leaving for Canada is both my son Fulì and my father Filippo. The same man seen on both sides of the lens, through binoculars. And his crossing begins. Mine too, in a sense. A triple crossing of memory. I am an absent father, a "being on paper," as were my sons, my grandsons, absent, and like my father and my grandfather, on paper as well. Dot by dot, my son disappears. My son in origami. Palermo, Genoa, Cannes, Barcelona, Lisbon. And three weeks later, he disembarks at Pier 21 in the port of Halifax, on that glacial day of April 1. Beginning a new life on April Fool's Day is something to think about. In reality, perhaps my son never left, he never turned up at the ferry terminal of Naples. Perhaps he just left in a dream, who knows, only abandoning his native home surrounded by vines and fruit trees to better enter the thick fog of his American fiction. Perhaps even some comic taped a jester on his back. All this is perhaps just a grotesque joke.

Chi dorme non piglia pesci, the Neapolitan proverb goes: "He who sleeps catches no fish." Don't waste time, Filippo, else you'll come to nothing and nothing will come to you, inevitably. Keep your eyes open, be attentive to what surrounds you. In our *paese* in Campania, they say that a fish is only a fish when it's thrown in the boat. In the water, it is no longer one, it will always be something else. They are happy there, because they are no longer fish, don't have a name, don't have to suffer the gaze of the Other. At the bottom of a boat or a fisherman's bucket, fish keep the suffocating memory of harsh light, of a wound on the mouth, a gash on the cheek. Far from your land, Fulì, you will change.

> *We are the products of a scene at which we were not present.*
> *Man is the creature who is missing an image.*
> —Pascal Quignard, *Sex and Terror*, tr. Chris Turner

While my grandfather was working in the countryside, a field rat, disturbed by his presence, I suppose, or to defend his parcel of territory, bit his hand. An amusing fact, the rodent didn't want to let go. However much my grandfather moaned, waving his hand in all directions, east west north south, at top speed, the rat still clung to the phalanx of his index finger. *Scarpe grosse cervello fino*. Big shoes perhaps, but shrewd. A good *cafóne*, normal reaction, he bit the rat in turn, directly on the neck, he clenched his teeth, so strongly, that the rat dropped dead. Another time, my grandfather fell from the chestnut tree he was pruning, having by error sawn the branch where he was indeed sitting. Filippo, my father, saw everything. He's the one who told me.

My father was not born to work the land, to wear himself out doing that. Very early on, he realized it. Then, one day, he declared to my grandfather he was no longer able to continue, to carry out the seasonal harvest of fruit, turning over the land, going to the market in Benevento at the foot of the hill, mules laden with these products of the land. His back aches were perhaps an excuse, but not his restless soul. He wanted to relax his muscles, his tendons, his nerves, that he had so often tensed, fists raised, to give a thrashing to the arrogant or to the offspring of other jealous landowners who were less well off than us, in terms of hectares of land, because honour called for it, because even among *terroni*, justice must be served. My father wanted to develop new areas, expand his field of activity. He had to pack his bags, turn his world around, break ties.

When he was young, he liked to watch the mountain that gently dominated his native region, the Sleeper of Sannio. It is named that as it calls to mind, from certain angles, a woman stretched out on her back in the middle of the valley. Between the female representation of the mountain and this territory where she is resting, a territory formerly occupied by the Samnites, one of the toughest Italic peoples of Antiquity, the contrast is striking. After standing up to Roman soldiers for centuries, and even humiliating them — the expression "to pass through the Caudine forks" stems from the Romans defeating them — the Samnite warriors finally had to abdicate, during the Battle of Benevento in 275 BC. At the time when Maleventum became Beneventum, where, in the head of the Romans who had seen in that an omen, the "Bad Event" became the "Good Event." This omnipresent sleeping lady of the valley gently recalls that.

"Listen, son. At school, they'll no longer call you a Wop. You're going to defend yourself now." As we rode on Boulevard Métropolitain, my father indicated with his finger the first of two identical buildings rising on rue Crémazie. "You see 3335? On the top floor, they give martial arts classes. The teacher's called Chang Soo Lee. An authority in Korean karate. You'll study with him, I registered you. Every Tuesday at seven p.m., I'll go with you. You'll defend yourself, my boy." I was eight years old, soon to be a yellow belt. And a bit of blood on my hands. The red stain on the snow adorning the schoolyard of Providence Sainte-Élisabeth came from Léonard's nose. That would teach him. He had his lesson. Because of karate classes, I missed all the episodes of *Batman* broadcast on CFCF 12 in the winter of 1968. On the other hand, I'd become, in the schoolyard, defender of the oppressed.

Twenty-nine clouds. At twenty-nine a man was in his thirtieth year. And he was twenty-nine.
—Malcolm Lowry, *Under the Volcano*

At the end of the Second World War, my son Fulì took a seat in the Rome-Express that provided the connection with Paris. During the journey, he had the opportunity to learn a new trade. A traveller loaned him *Handbook for Becoming a Welder*, which he read in one go between the Eternal City and the City of Light, lulled by the rolling of the train. In this convoy bringing him from one bombarded point to another in a Europe to reconstruct, between two imaginary stations, my son learned to become a welder, to weld train cars. Later, in Montreal, he would work for CN and CP. It really is amazing. It is like sawing the branch on which we are sitting. Biting the rat who bites us. Throwing the net of memories into the water to hoist yourself inside the boat. Joining the swarming mass of migrants gathered on the quay while the sound of a siren envelops the entire port area, the departure call for the *Homérique* is heard.

▲▲▲

This man who was not yet thirty began little by little to disappear. That was his wish, to be reborn with his wild heart. He disappeared progressively from one point to another in the ocean to live life-size at the other end of the world. It could have been in Argentina, in Australia, but it was in Canada. He finally disembarked in Montreal. Gathering strength from his Paris experience and drawing confidence in his knowledge of French, although basic, he intended to build something — a house, a business, a long poem in verse, a narrative.

Thanks to the immersion experience, he would have less and less on the tip of the tongue the words *pesce* (fish), *scarpa* (shoe). They would all shine henceforth. They'd be wriggling catches. A still intangible woman waited on the other shore, a job, a future, who knows, a family to conceive, a tree to plant in North America. My son entered his new life. It is like progress in the passing of seasons, a law of implacable nature.

Dramatic Increase in Signs

THE ORIGIN OF THE FUTURE takes root in the fear of famine, in the recurring vision of a herd of cattle pushed to the edge of a ravine. Will we end up arriving, though we don't know the place we come from? Where will we continue to go now? In this forest of harmonious abundance, in this hotel of hostilities where what falls to us makes us more sensitive, we hold you, land of plenty widening out, alternating break-ups, as if being part of a Whole, unequivocal, for we are wild berries set out in bunches at the edge of an arm of hydrogen turning blue. Circles of space, achene pecked at by the state of nature, from the wapiti have we not inherited a sixth sense? We enter the forest whose attraction grows the way you enter a divided kingdom. In the richness of wood, each tree is a half-open door you push with your foot to enter somewhere discreetly, silently, and dispute there in seclusion our due, our survival.

And perpendicularly its smoke will carry in the sky
The message of the approach,
through all the mountain passes,
Of a new rush of bisons.
—Jean-Aubert Loranger, *Terra Nova*

Are we so far
from the mountain to climb?
—Joséphine Bacon, *Bâtons à message / Tshissinuatshitakana*

You want to come see to observe, with your own eyes, how obscure the absolute is, dismiss the abstraction and hammer this matter that strews the earth where we shirk? We would like to see you lend an ear when the fauna proclaims its original hymns, we'd like that, in the face of this insurmountable spectacle that offers to the first comers such a flight of flying specimens to delight you.

▲▲▲

As shrewd as it is authentic, snuggling against the splendid flatness of the taiga, a bowl filled with crackling idleness at the end of a pipe, faces the colour of bran, my people go to the vision by the shortest path.

As far as a shower of the brush, we return scorned, black magic in our heads, having not chased what? A thousand-year-old deflected meteorite.

When the chinook blows from the Rockies rolling its totems to here, when lying in wait for the white noise spread by the moss, our bodies turn around, a full pouch of sea foam in the soul, toward the North, do you think we rejoice, that we really hold ourselves in place?

Our people advance beneath a boreal dome. They gather their propitiatory game at the foot of the stars. Its long smooth hair, black like obsidian, recalls what remained of a craft of weaving forgotten in the forest after thirty thousand years of plant life.

From where does so much insistence to reach the South come to us like a pearl of sweat? Of the glaciers only a thin groove scarcely visible remains in the creaking memory of lakes. On these green shores where we bivouac, time is still needed for the rubber to sweat, for the mango to turn orange, certainly. We are still short of the mezcal of our Aztec brothers. On the other hand, the time of famine is good when, lying under a leafy beech tree, we become the shaded extension of its roots.

> Would you believe it if I told you that our aspiration was growing in these lands where so much fruit grows on the edge of pulpy rapids, where at streams angoras with infinite pelisses still drink, their gaze even more timid? To this aspiration that has precedence, our souls have moulded themselves, and as our moccasins lag rhythmically on the snow, to these bent lands we lend a rhythm that they send back to us a hundredfold. Yet, one day, will you reach these ochre shores, will you hear our supernatural music and will you eat in our bowls. Will you slip comforted in our skins, will you quench your thirst in the hollow of our hands, and perhaps that is well, for from everywhere and for a long time, the roads roaming around here meander.

Then, waiting, idle like geese, we sculpt small branches with a knife or throw pebbles in a lake and they create wreaths. During this time, the trickster decked out in old reindeer antlers, tattooed to the marrow of irreconcilable beasts, imagines himself here planting wigwams as essential as the Pyramid of Cheops.

In the shape of a circle life circulates and in the same way emerges through a curve. From the start, is the moon the arc extended as far as it can, eclipsed by the arm of an archer? Does the sun twirl around in the air, a saffron eagle that no arrow grazes? Without an answer, we will still dance in a circle amid the smoke, to the stupefying sound of drums and rattles, carried by braids of light, burning from above, we will rise to the oldest and farthest doodle of stars, we will run far thanks to an elastic slender leg stretched to the max and that leads up to the Big Crunch theory.

It will be during a pow-wow, among the forceful sounds and circular tam-tams that we will choose to return to the globe, to sound the knell, when from inaction will shoot forth swarms of dreams, and equipped with this only this baggage, we will forage identical flora at the ends of the earth.

▲▲▲

Here everything profits. The flowers. The storm. The souls. Love and the wolverine profit. The ruses of the racoon profit, and they resist. Even the dykes of our brave beavers hold firm to the rhythm of the rivers, to cascades of blue sky. Of our brave beavers! … Let us forgive them as they leave their hiding places for all the lead that one day you'll stick into their skin! And all that nickel! And the world turns again, still, leads us in the dance, in a circle, while we nod our heads, while our fingers drum in opposite directions on all given surfaces, and our gods positioned in the doorway walk their big shoes on the polar circle that we would crush for less.

▲▲▲

Pre-Columbian, pre-Cortes, pre-Cabot, pre-Verrazano, pre-Catalan, these faraway strangers have jumped into the spirit of the day, and by pure chance, ended up in the history of others. Were they white as talc? Aboard machines tailed by pirates of antimatter constructed in their own image, men with gleaming helmets inset with horns, a crown of red hair signing a hyperbola at their jaw, disembark with a decided step on the shores of this already-seen. Full of questionable drive, on the red sand, they approached the town intact and, quite simply, made contact.

Vikings whose boat named "longship" in your jargon know better than our own the key of the seas, why do you not come? Why do you not set down the squares of fur that cover you, form a flaccid armour when you throw them at your feet? Why not put down the sword and assuage your search for ridged space in this heartrending bear bite, these lapping of fawns, this skewered fresh-water salmon that turn a wonderful pink on the fire?

We keep you alive like the fire. As if it were one of our women, we will respect your line. Why not relieve yourself of this perilous journey, revel in this bed of fir? We are not trying to pick a quarrel with you who, facing the ocean, hoisted the sails without ever looking back. Vikings! Why don't you come? Why don't you put down your drenched irons and park beneath that tree your no less amazing canoes?

And that evening, when the Moon has countered the Sun, our people will serve a banquet. The clan will be all ears to enjoy your heroic songs destined for Odin's Valhalla. It will dream of the new delights that, Thor or Woden, your presence will arouse in it. Exhausted, you will finally reach our teepees calculating perhaps that your people and ours sail the same waters.

When you moor in the never-named haven, we detected in you a grandeur of soul as deep, delimited as a former glacier transformed into a lake.

> Is there a crossing that is in vain if it turns out that the thirst for space leads the heart of the newcomer to recognize a nation different from what it is? And the hearts of Erik the Red's subjects appeared more generous than the sea, when even the sea could have had in store, we realize, unexpected presents.

Do we swoon before these born navigators who know how to love and wage war with equal ardour, and when with him, blond Norseman, nearby Scandinavian, we play games of skill, did you know that there is never conqueror or defeated? The wisdom of the territory is contained implacably in this goatskin and like the smallest stream will one day throw itself in the sea, we will quench your thirst thanks to this thermal flask.

Vikings! Come! Array yourself with our insignia, combat the forces of nature, come net fishing with us, melt iron, exchange and make harpoons that will be effective. You will build ovens able to redden on its platform the complete age of polished stone. In this spacious place where patience is mellow, wisdom is pensive, you will plant your home, wigwam on our earth, learn to make snowshoes, to prepare the batiscan.

With you, will we form other intense alliances? Odin's paradise had half-reached us, when, with blood a bit diluted, our people launched themselves to attack a whole new era. Did our wildfowl cook that much, as you no doubt believed, on the icebergs drifting slowly beneath the April sun off of Newfoundland?

> And one day, the village of souls shifted, instilling a drizzle of blood in our hair and the Viking tribe unexpectedly went away. What did it leave it its wake? For each trace, runic stones flourished very high in a Vinland valley, isolated once again.

▲▲▲

Our women are the best pillars of the clan. We advance this hypothesis. The uncles on the maternal side have the same power on their offspring as the Moon on the ebbing tides. We believe it. Also, let us leave a universal womb, arrow-case shifting on the shoulder blade, to reach the clan of another female while pursuing, not saying a word, the smell of a trout. In our mothers less melancholy than moody, we had to enter to one day hope to leave.

It was at twilight, usually, after a corn stew, around the fire sticking out its tongues, that with the bone needle they sew our attire or, to alleviate the cries of fear lying in wait for them, they chew, crouching, leather that tastes like the earth. In the evenings they crush, in the cavity of mortars, the seedlings they had spread at dawn. In the absence of men propelled at the end of a sling into hunting parties, they will make bundles of wood that will warm the winter. Coiffed in a cloud of ultrasound, they will sew the necessary *watap*, tan the skins, brush the skunk fur, knead earth and bannock, turn their backs to war while regularly cuddling their chubby-cheeked papooses. In addition, they'll wash in groups of six or seven, naked in the creeks, bead moccasins, dresses, take snuff and mix the oatmeal. With just one wink at the wildlife, they have the power to shoot the game for an entire season, that they will then skin, eyes closed. Is it true that people listen to them religiously, inside or outside the Councils? In holophrastic discussions, they know in practice how to flush out the geniuses. But when, corn on their minds, in their twilight years, they move toward the universal secret, we naturally silence their names. Where do they came from? Where do they go, these names? And all these words in succession, do they really exist?

▲▲▲

Completely clear, enigmatic selenic crater, our government is worthy of your hooded torturers. A spider with an orange abdomen has spun webs in the system in which, since the purest meteorites have rained down on the earth, we settle our differences with the Sagamos. This principle is simple. The unit contains the multiple and the multiple the unit. Is it really that? Is that the forerunner of the Charter of Human Rights and Freedoms? If the dividing line between our so-called savage peoples seems finer than the spider's thread, in the end, it's because everything belongs to everyone and nothing belongs to anyone.

On our merciless lands, the soul of a murderer could not run very far if that of the murdered, more volatile than an evil spell or the gas in a Zippo lighter, followed it everywhere humanly possible for an incriminated soul to find refuge and tranquility. Is there no jail more unfit or gorge or mass grave that alone can hide all the wrongs of one sole man?

Here, we punish the crime and not the criminal. Here, everyone is a writer and no one creates literature. That's why our poor scatterbrain, to whom chase was duly given by a corpse and by stillborn words, will pay to the tearful family a conventional string of wampum with sincere messages. But once the sorrow of each one is purged, is it said somewhere that the village will once again become free in equilibrium?

▲▲▲

Our healers are not the only ones to know bleeding and suction. Didn't blood-sucking mosquitoes, even in the swamps in the shadow of Hippocrates, on a small scale, already put this into practice a long time ago?

Even though the spontaneous oaths given by medicine men and trances intertwine, we enter, eyes closed and all the same, a waiting room, while maintaining a respect for the handfuls of medicinal plants pulled up in the heath that is at least equal to that of the swan song.

Death is supposedly moribund. Isn't that a good sign? For that, our plumed witches, past masters in the art of reaching the beyond, assure us they can revive it.

War is a Wreckhouse wind blowing on the dozing body of a batrachian. Is war really an axe driven into the cortex of the brain, a murder traumatizing us, a border that expands? When a corpse washes its dismembered body in a stream, do we ever see a hyena rushing up more quickly this surreal metaphor, or across from it, laugh more grudgingly? A dirty war, quite obviously, can never guarantee the hygiene of nations. But in our forest of conifers and birches, revolt is brewing — do you hear this bass between the broad-leaved trees? — and it is in no way our responsibility to repress it.

▲▲▲

Were we the naïve creatures going by parallel worlds, a laced purse filled with tobacco by our side, seeking secrets that covet your animism? A breeze blew the way a swearword is slipped onto the slimy back of a bullfrog. One day, the idea of a raid will touch the spirit's mind and it will raise its axes immediately between our scattered nations, weaved with old relationships. Nothing here is more beautiful, after a punitive expedition, than returning to the village by a maze of paths stained with a very light-coloured AB positive, when the tufts of the enemy raised like a scarecrow at the end of a pole still dangle fresh and bloody scalps.

Pulling the axe from the case of a skull, launching into the pursuit of intertribal redemption. Are the stimuli missing? Do we avenge death, that's it, that's all, is that really all? Some speak of homeopathy, later, while it is really about a famous deletion of the Other, if it is not actually a deletion of nature. Do warriors display faces painted with invisible chlorophyl that before long their women, in a group, suffer from the forced divorce caused by these erectile departures. Will the law of the strongest return to the fold? They think so, salivating.

When we return to the village, bothered by glimpses of victories, war trophies trailing behind us, the question of the hour remains to know until when our prisoners, intrepid interlacing of love and psyche, will endure the torture automatically imposed upon them.

> *I know not whether Your Paternity will recognize the handwriting of a poor cripple, who formerly, when in perfect health, was well known to you. The letter is badly written, and quite soiled, because, among other inconveniences, the writer has but one whole finger on his right hand, and can scarcely prevent the paper's being stained by the blood which flows from his yet unhealed wounds. His ink is arquebuse powder [gunpowder rubbed up with water], and his table the bare earth. He writes to you from the land of the Iroquois, where he is now a captive [...]*
>
> —Francesco Giuseppe Bressani, *Captives Among the Indians*

Is there anything more poignant to hear at the end of a dark forest than a war song struck up by a prisoner twisted on a crimson scaffold? The courage of captives makes it a point of honour to shout; through that we must conclude how the weapon was grasped. The shell of a zebra mussel can also do the trick. The index finger and the baby finger are favoured. In that order. Then come the ring and the middle finger. That squirts red and quite far, but only the body is stained, rarely the soul. They do not touch the thumb, in case, and between phalanxes, middle phalanxes and distal phalanxes, an array of angels would fly away where many scales take shape and are inserted. All permutations are allowed, setting the nerves of the captives on edge. If that one has a hard life, we adopt him. Isn't that the driving principle of any nation that respects itself?

FOURTH MOVEMENT: WIND

The Desert

I DON'T HAVE THE WORDS. Nor am I all-knowing. My language is not precise. All my certainties waver. It's not because of French. All languages are on equal footing. I go with the words and phrases available, those that first pass beneath my door left unwatched. The words still don't exist. They have not yet emerged, or have not yet returned. Stuck against the inner wall of a cave, a stomach, a helium balloon, like an echo, or remaining before the front door, words difficult to incorporate. I make do with what I have in my head, what's within arm's reach. One thing is clear in any case. My face is the stage for an attack of acne. I put on nothing other than T-shirts of bands, and only if they are black. I identify with them, in dark tones, and these bands are Bad Religion, Dag Nasty, SNFU, Fugazi, Descendents, Face to Face, NOFX. This summer, the record shops are my most frequent place to hang on my afternoons without end. I'll also go to X20 to compare the Vans, try on pants, have a look at the posters.

The last semester at Collège de Montréal has not yet ended and I have my hair tinted lime green. We decided that together, Guillaume and I. Fanny's mother is a hairdresser. First she bleached us, then dyed our hair. We're absolutely gorgeous. At any rate, it's flashy. Really nice. Normally, I'm brown-haired. With my red and black striped pants, like a kilt, my Nils T-shirt, hair to my shoulders, with that look, I make an impact. When I pass by the mirror, I see in myself the features of a Navajo or a Hopi. That's my way of doing my own thing, of standing out, of being looked at oddly. I adore being looked at oddly. To be honest, I don't give a damn about how others look at me. Fuck the world. Do it yourself, man.

▲▲▲

With my mother's authorization, my father, a knowledgeable Dairy Queener, has taken off the last two weeks of July. It's good to hold down the fort during the heat, in Rosemont, and when it's my Uncle Fred and the staff defending the northwest flank, it's even better. Dad likes road trips, like me. His pleasure on the road he probably gets from his father. When he was little, Filippo and Suzanne would take him to Florida every winter. They did the trip by Cadillac. They'd join my grandmother's brother, Gaston, and his wife Lina who owned two DQs in Montreal, as well as a pied-à-terre in Fort Lauderdale. The entire Quebec jet set in the 1960s would meet up in Miami. In an old black and white photo with a light border, my father is at the beach, a chubby four-year-old sitting on the tanned knees of a young and beautiful woman, very beautiful even, and glowing. My father told me that it was Lise Watier before the Cosmetics, her lips visibly coated in a cream to hydrate them. My grandfather liked Florida, but not to settle there permanently for the winter. He still thought of his *paese* in Italy, I imagine. He dreamed of returning there, yet my grandmother didn't see things the same way. She was shy, attached to her American roots, her family, even if it had fragmented. She never became infatuated with Filippo's little village, which appeared to her distant and backward — understandably so, it was 1956! — compared to the larger and more grounded one that Montreal was in those days. Apparently once my grandfather sensed a good bargain and almost bought himself a hotel on the island of Ischia, in Campania. But, when it comes to anecdotes, the one to really ask is my father.

At the last minute, my family opted for the southwestern United States. I still wonder if I'll go there. I'm thinking of that, very softly, condemned to go round in circles with the soul of words, to wander, to dance in my kiva, my ceremonial chamber, fly like an eagle in the sun. I'm going, I'm not going. The decision-making of a strategist. July is a dead month, friends don't really know what to do when the heatwave hits Montreal, and I hate swimming. The parents set out the program. They did everything online, reservations, airplane, hotels from Protoexpedia or Paleotrivago. That's the first time they reserved from home, without moving.

In short, we'll fly Montreal-Phoenix. Fine. Before accepting, I weighed the pros and cons. The cons: my parents as such, of course. Their long conversations in the car, their drama. I wonder why it takes so many words to arrive at point x, although, on the other hand, I can fall back on music, increase the volume, forget about everything. Inside the car, they usually listen to their Talking Heads, generally with joy, singing, or to Frank Zappa, to Detroit or minimal techno. Occasionally I put a CD in the reader or listen to music in by headphones and by that action, it's myself I'm burying. I bury myself, shut myself away. With little shovelfuls of swift earth, I disappear, burrow myself, in an unrestrained series of pieces that I memorize, that I accompany with the sticks of my fingers on everything that's offered as a surface. All surfaces are skins offered to my ears, in any case.

I also place in the balance the rhythm imposed by a whirlwind journey, having to rise early, breakfasts in a rush. Driving in the desert, raising some dust, swallowing tons of kilometres mentally, advancing on a pure line, it's all the same, it's the lot of any road traveller. In this kind of click trip, each second counts, there's very little time at our disposal, or to lose. And this question reiterated daily, what are we going to eat? Where? Should we make a stop? Where? Why not at the Waffle House? Please, the Waffle House.

One thing, however, carried weight in my decision making. It's this fantastic idea of Googling "show, punk rock, west coast." I saw that Big Drill Car was doing the first part of the All at the House of Blues in San Diego, on July 21. And on July 21, we "were supposed to be" in "the" area. Once this six hundred-kilometre detour of to the west was negotiated with the parents, I bought the idea, without hesitating, without even spending a cent, except for the price of the entrance ticket to the show. I'd stand my ground. The United States obtained Louisiana for five million dollars, I'd buy my parents with a little detour via California. Never would I have given up this road trip for all the gold in the West.

▲▲▲

The myth of the border occurs rather close beneath our feet, on this side of the Appalachians, where today airliners criss-cross constantly. The Cincinnati Airport. Stop off. Stopover. Cowboy boots and hats, teak furniture in the waiting areas, the bars, the concourse. Professor Jetté's history class resurfaces. What are the main points of friction in North America just before the English conquest? Acadie, the south of Lake Champlain and the Ohio Valley, mainly. Ohio, around 1750, was the key to the continent for the French and the Anglos. It opened onto Louisiana, which the old counties later returned to one another like a beach ball. It was an open gate to wage the War of Independence. I know all that, had prepared myself for the provincial exam. And my father signed the contract for the car rental, a white Ford Taurus with a sliding roof to let in the Sun King, circulate the smells of tauromachy, letting out the pheromones abundantly emitted by the *Cactus erectus*.

When my mother drives the Taurus, my father sets down poems in his notebook, in handwriting that is liquid and bewitching, he's evidently developing some research, speaks to us of Zanzotto, Sanguineti, Balestrini, poets that he reads and names that remind me of those of insects, I remember only the wind, a wind of freedom. I read this line by Carl Sandburg, "Freedom is cheap," in a book lying around in back, and I like it. We arrive at Apache Junction, pass Tortilla Flat, move forward on the Apache Trail, the route is windy and narrow, we quietly leave what was already a tiny bit of civilization where we rode to wrap ourselves, above, in nature, in the fissure, on a road that literally snakes among stone, the land, moss, the desert roses, the nopals, the saguaros.

Nothing before had appeared so magical to me. The blondness of the green landscapes is breathtaking, the Canon cameras delighted in it, turning their attention to the mental reconstitution of the Grand Canyon, with minimal techno music by Plastikman in the background, through the sliding roof I watch a saffron eagle in gliding flight. As my father would say, it turns, taking itself for a sun before Copernicus, its wings spread wide, it is the very image of free will, of harmony incarnate, of peace, of fulfillment gathered in one sole point that surveys the Apache Trail, for *nihil, idem, ante rem*, as my father says. For the thrill of gliding.

▲▲▲

Adopt a Highway, that's the best thing we have to do now, en route to San Diego, among these landscapes of the ends the earth, of history, of man, of the end of territories. Ride a highway, ride along this pure line that is a bridge, a viaduct or a road, back in the day a rite. With a half tank of gas we cross through disappeared pueblos and Indian reserves, mini-counters coloured with Navajo artefacts spread out here and there in the large spaces of a small universe, painted deserts, petrified tree trunks, pueblos living on mesas, in homes built with adobe.

As we were crossing the desert, I dozed off on the damp seat. I had this strange dream. I am dancing in a *kiva* and watch an Indian, a Navajo sweep by the Navajo nation, at the wheel of the last vehicle to come out of General Motors factory in Sainte-Thérèse on August 27, 2002, a Chevrolet Camaro Z28, his is red — proof that we dream in colour, that we notice ourselves dreaming in colour. I see dust falling, flashes. I see employees from the Zuni road department re-asphalting the road, surfacing it, covering the desert with another layer of tar and feathers. Men of few words, the dreamlike Comanches, happy, throw dust in the eyes of their modified Thunderbird. I am depressed. I bring back Mormons playing checkers above a chessboard taken from the motherland, moving their checkered pioneers. The rented Taurus, doomed for the carwash, charges into this gigantic game of snakes and ladders that is the landscape. The sun, incredible, is reflected everywhere on its white metal body. Through desiring the blond-green desert, become ochre after miles and miles of road, the earth's monuments manage to hold on only by a balancing wire, by a thin border no one has yet established between the material, spiritual and geomorphic worlds. The breath of the Spirit can bring down on Antelope Mesa castles in Spain, paper forts, evangelizing missions, surrounded as always by mega-cracking of stone, like the one that struck during the eruption of the Sunset crater and that shook the current zone of Flagstaff in 1085.

I open my eyes and we arrive in San Diego. The car is like a music box, a skateboard rolling in the white city and its maze. The show takes place this evening. My father stubbornly insists on attending this great California celebration, I understand him, I'm not opposed. He'll be in the orchestra where alcoholic beverages are allowed, and I and those who are not twenty-one, forbidden to buy alcohol, will be perched in the balcony, on our elevated plateaux, left to our vibrations.

Big Drill Car smash in with their catchy melodies. They redo *Big Shot* by Billy Joel. I'm in heaven. The All follow. Their drummer is one of my idols. He's overweight, but that takes nothing away from his playing. Right now, he strikes incredibly, as quick as a flash, with millimetric precision. I adore his drumming. My mother, Carolina F., didn't come in. She remained in front of the bar doors, had to make a phone call to Italy, first. She spent the show outside, seated on the doorstep of the House of Blues, chatting with the owner of the famous bar. No doubt he cruised her, confessed to her that he loved Rome, blablabla. My father finds that the singer of The All looks just like Valerio Magrelli. Valerio Magrelli, who is that, already? Oh yes, it's his friend the Roman poet.

▲▲▲

Dreams, once satisfied, have no more tangible direction or place to go. It's like a flat tire. Either you replace it or you stop. After India, the Border, Eldorado, Paradise, the Indians, the earthquakes, Silicon Valley, Palo Alto, after that line, what is there? What remains of the Southwest? The desert? Who's left when the show is over? No one. A resonance. An echo. I don't know what pushes me to continue. But I continue, day after day. I am and I follow the rhythm, the revolution of the wheels, like "wandering" toward the South thous, this sandy mouth of the South, where each cactus unhurriedly but surely marks the way, since geological times. Better to turn off toward this other gold, the North, arrived at the edge of the Pacific and its fog banks.

When nothing more is sure or a source of wonder, when the future is blocked, fortunately there is chance. We were returning on foot from Fisherman's Wharf in San Francisco, amid the bleating sea lions on Pier 39, with the island of Alcatraz in the background, when I came across the singer from the Sainte Catherines, a Montreal hardcore punk group. The singer is with his girlfriend and their two young children. I eagerly follow anything to do with punk rock, so I know they signed a contract with a California label. He's no doubt in San Francisco for business. He even invented a dish, Pouzza, poutine and pizza in one, I don't know if he has a registered trademark, but I know it will inspire the creation of Pouzza Fest, a Montreal festival. Still incredulous, I exchange a few words with him, it's too cool.

Hilly Frisco. Cliffs rich in minerals. The streetcars leap from one hill to another, with us inside, then we go by foot along Jack Kerouac Alley between City Lights Bookstore and Vesuvio Café, where I am refused access because of my age. San Francisco Bay, the Bay of Naples, is almost the same bay, linking together a fault, the San Andreas, and a volcano, Vesuvius. On the other side of the Golden Gate, perky white sharks go berserk in their own magnetic field. I await the next words like a surfer awaits the adequate wave. I take it. After that wave, that line, nothing more.

The Foundations of the South

And then? Return to the Atlantic Ocean. At once rolling, rough, solemn and gravid, a "pregnant" ocean. The trade winds have pushed the conquistadors on new curls of salt to here. The three caravels pitch quite simply on waves of liquid gold, still. Inclined to give birth, dear ocean. To whom? To what? You roll so well that the calm flat sea glimmers, and every day it's marvellous to see this turquoise, this emerald, this topaz, this cobalt blue. Three wrecks in the distance as if set out to dry in the air of violence. This territory on which Spain counted is a jungle without gems, with the pearls of a broken necklace fallen from the neck of the ouroboros. It is a world whose circle was believed to be completed for a peccadillo. Seeking a passage that would enclose the Atlantic while being favourable to it, a population of ibises, perhaps lost, black riders, treasure seekers, carried in the hollow of a shell, approached by the shortest way the detected shores of my ancestral continent. Would you like some more coffee? How many sugars was that?

Even if it's true, it's false.
—Henri Michaux, *Face aux verrous*

Small islands of migratory geese emerge from the mouth of the great river to the floating city of Tenochtitlán, where the sun, when setting, is a ripe fruit falling from its branch, where the monarch butterfly, to reach without landing, must beat its wings no less three hundred million times. And the three hundred and fifty-two Mi'kmaw paddlers, driven back at the antepenultimate junction of the rivers, what will become of them?

It appears that a few additional portage moons will suffice to lead them deep into the Aztec forest first, then into the Mayan city, built secretly on high. A day of ductile brightness, like gold, the light extending to such a point that it could break off and release all the real, our faithful shaman, haruspex of the clan, appears bathed in sweat and spreads everywhere the rumour of this disappointment: the rather disconcerting discovery occurred farther down in the Caribbean Sea.

▲▲▲

You recovered so well from your first weakness that thanks to a sovereign of Spain, you immediately gave to this explicit setting the unanalyzable name of San Salvador. Their island was cut off beneath their feet like when you suddenly pull off a tablecloth and there remains only the egg of Christopher Colombus on the table, and on the ground a few extinguished cigarillos in the icing of a mille-feuille, chipped plates, Cuba libre spilled on the terrazzo. They had discovered fraud, an old Freudian dream, their fallibility confined to record levels in the Guanahani stock market in the lean years, too lean, that they fell flat before this full stop.

> The sea often gives birth to strange guests. The mother-of-pearl encrusted in the shells practised recording your amazement and our own.

Your caravels come from periscope Europe progress toward them, they moor a stone's throw from this beach of cruelly blond sand. A standard raised, in the distance the masts of the Niña arose in the sky that they prickled like bamboo, stalks of sugarcane.

From a crack in the eggshell, historiated, archived men, accompanied by a notary, sprang, armed with their wisdom of fencing, of the cross, of the arquebus. As numerous as the spawn of the swordfish, like an ocean entered into a sponge, the men cast poorly enlightened glances.

Beneath disproportionate cumuli, foamy, pasteurized, skimmed, recalling the old man and the sea, your foot finally touched the water, creating a shower of drops remaining frozen on the horizon. Did you notice it?

Cristoforo Colombo, is it really you, native of Genoa, from the thighs of a Castilian Isabella? The inhabitants of the island greedily swallowed your multi-faceted knowledge of go-between. Despite this very first step, you have no privilege over this innocent world where only the new, the exoticism and the ferocity astound you.

Remember that, as the crow flies, for those who spend their life in the air, distances are much shorter than by boat. And yet … You landed like the shell of a nut on the water, a coconut fallen from a royal palm on the sinciput of the West.

Colombus found India where he wanted it to be and there it was, filled with luxuriant signs. At the end of the rolling Caribbean Sea, weighted in a halo of aquamarine water, he wrongly thought himself the lottery winner of a two-week all-inclusive stay.

In the distance, like a field of corn, the masts of the Niña nibbled the mango-coloured sky. Wrong way, false hunger, false shine. Vain hopes come to mow us down hard. Blazing seabird, Latin veil flapping in the wind for the Iberian cause, pale, your face appeared to us on this side of the mirror.

And in your sumptuous yellow, red and blue salons, decorated with damask fabrics and chessboards from which you dreamt up the world, in your apartments flowing with curtains where through wide openings the view of campaniles elevated your soul to make it burst, we left you to invent as you wished one world and another, and another, and another, over and over again.

We did not hold back the hand that caressed your dream. But now, convince your flashy companions to take up again muskets, sabres, chains, crucifixes, armour, then with some Hispanic sign, command them to turn back.

If the South hypnotizes you so, we urge you to consult your cards again, for the castles that will collapse here are not made up of playing cards, but plated with gold leaf. Laurentian hunters, wapiti, whitetail deer and magnetic pole, we Wendat, Mohawk or Wabanaki, united to fight blizzards, frostbite, invaders, whatever they may be, are incapable of inventing a justification to our symbolic decapitation. Around the fire we slowly describe how the climate in Andalusia acts on your complexion and makes it less light than that of the Scandinavian sailors, the memory of whom remains intact in our hearts. Let's hope that when the colour spectrum is activated you read our skin correctly. Is it because it is hirsute that your face repels us? It's not a judgment, but we know that once pushed to the limit, in a crisis of anger, the piggybank broken, you could certainly reduce us to nothing.

> The head of your god is probably not feathered. In his
> eyes sparkle neither quartz nor obsidian. In his chest
> too often the sun has disowned the moon.

This is a warning to the reader of signs that you are. Do not venture to enter this rocky shield of prickly conifers. Other men will come, today or tomorrow, rubbing themselves against our wild brambles. Choose your paradise on that line below, in the thermal gardens where, one after the other, the bell-shaped flowers of guaiacums and yuccas open. Choose it amid the banana plantations, the papaya and mango trees. Keep your hell for the Indios. Don't you see that they're ready to cross machetes?

▲▲▲

We have only to think of Cortès christening Veracruz, another atopic land, and our faces flush. He had India, that conquistador, inscribed around his head as if it were an outfitter. To say that having confused him with Quetzalcóatl, we introduced him to the splendour of our temples. A case of mistaken identity, when this person is God, obviously does not forgive.

> Is it possible that your god did not recognize us immediately? Is it possible that a god can miss the boat?
>
> The hideousness of this hoax grovels in the selva.
>
> The ocean, this statistical probability of conquests, this conveyor belt for conquistadors, that you very often contemplated from the high towers of Salamanca, now arrives at your feet, the Ocean, without condition, without effort, almost without blushing from its unfurling. Like a jealous king whose accumulated gold only manages to pay a bit of his debt, did you flout its routes and its rites, did you take the machete to slip among the iguanas to the swamp? In the marshes travelled by alligators you exclaimed

"*hace mucho calor*" but all that was a sham, because
really you were entering the universe of a race to mow
it down at its roots.

Among our neighbours there grows a native species of peyote, totally adorable, and despite the fires lit here and there in the recesses of roomy dreamlike alcoves, we shrewdly assume these things that our visions infiltrated with words, buds, abbeys graze upon.

The irremediable happens to us brutally through air, sea or land, things seen in turn look at us from an identical eye. May the *leaves of grass*, turned like cold antenna toward the greyness where our fir trees stand tall, preserve in their soul the spiritual animal on which we depend, of which our amulets bear the portrait. Watching is required night and day at the top of our green miradors.

Did you melt its gold into ingots because your economy was doing poorly? Did you sully its integrity in an amused and Eurocentric upsurge? Did you pillage its cities, rape its daughters, in the name of a god, of a king to which we are deaf? Had it not been for the good Las Casas and a famous papal bull that still embarrasses us, we would hardly be worth more in your minds veiled in tulle than a few exotic four-legged creatures coming and going in a cage beneath the unruffled human eye.

In a field abundant with corn, we see instead the hands
of all our people turned toward the furfuraceous sun.

Majestic horse, model of grace between the jaws. With just one whinny, rearing up just once, you conquered the already enslaved heart of our men. Equine of iniquity, undivided rock, you cast a widening shadow on the town square. Must you, for your trouble, endure the death of a black knight on a white square? Oh, horse! On your saddle did a pommel suddenly appear so that the Spaniard can hang onto it, Catholic! Did he lead you to America in good faith? If only his aims had been noble! An athletic stallion stamping nervously in a cloud of gold dust and noticing in Taxco seven silver hippodromes standing in lieu of baroque cathedrals. Weapon with no intention to slay anyone, you reared up in the infinite, breathing out through your race cars with as much horsepower. Later, the horse turned against you when the brave Comanches, jumping on this opportunity where the Pueblos rose up, managed to bring under control four hundred mustangs, to change them, to have them move along the seafront promenade in Hispaniola.

▲▲▲

Like a voracious bird of prey standing, plumage with concentric reflections, with little terse jumps in the middle of a game of pelote you've jumped on them, snapping your beak. Do you see these lamb faces frown in the empire's antechamber? They are, as my friend the Roman poet said, fighting lambs.

You followed the trail of tears to return to your loved one and snatch them away. Your gaze quells the Andean condors. The source of the nectar for which you thirst basically doesn't matter to you.

You dangled before them a paradise shining at the end of your blood. You thought they would portray this interminable intrigue, but you seemed to forget that a real Greek tragedy ends when the chorus withdraws.

> Chac-Mool reclining in an omen, his own urn providing cyclical time when the event replays, returns,

> rolls like wheel in cosmogony. As for Christian time, doesn't it strive more towards apotheosis, historic, unidirectional light, as after 1492 come 1493, 1494, 1495 and so on? Two times face off. An arrow planted in the spoke the wheel of a stagecoach.

Aren't you a vulture like the others? Can it be you're trafficking in the theft of a man's body?

▲▲▲

You will see, our docile brothers will hide away in monastic silence at the time of a piquant solar eclipse. Slumming it, they'll keep turning in circles from one monumental valley to the next, going back to the Four Corners, a geometric nothing. But the Día de los Muertos will come, they'll remove their poncho and with this cochineal at the end of their fingers, old unappeased papal desire, they will skilfully dress the rebel souls of Pancho Villa and Emiliano Zapata.

Returning to your tomb of petulant conquistador, your decalcified skeleton will see itself forced to reconstruct letters patent and worn-out contracts, without which in a merciless combat our supposedly docile brothers will take on the aspect of eagles in full flight, then, supported by the mouth of the volcanoes Popocatépetl and Iztaccíhuatl kissing, after a shower of slow meteorites, they'll recover independence and freedom in an explosion of joy.

▲▲▲

You look us in the whites of the eyes. We see only the eyes of a White man. We consider you with our eyes. For us you have no consideration. You urge us to cooperate. In fact, you kill us through our souls and our bodies. You make a religious sign to us. In fact, you bleed us religiously.

At the foot of a wooden gallows with a crossbeam, you let yourself fall heavily to your kneecaps. Would it have been better for you to erase India from your cortex? You say you sailed close to the winds, treaded in a world of dreams that your sovereigns hoped was round, don't give a damn, you killed two birds with one stone. Would the gold of your *Conquista* have been too soft without this alloy of violence, of ferocity, of barbarity?

FIFTH MOVEMENT: HISTORY

For Anecdotal history

I was born Geneviève Clarisse Messier. In Saint-Charles-de-Lachenaie, in 1891. I am the wife of Ernest Rénaldi Lippé. There is an acute accent on the e of my last name. That was added by a grandfather in the line of descent, to Frenchify the German pronunciation — that grandfather must have been very tired of hearing Anglophones constantly pronouncing his name Italian style, Lippi; as for the acute accent on Rénaldi, it's to Canadianize the Italian Rinaldo, I suppose. In any case, my husband was conspicuous by his absence, he too. Just like Ti-Pouce's other grandfather, the one on the Catalano side, the Samnite of Beneventum, who was never ever there at the right time — and who, according to what I was told, sitting on his chestnut tree, strove hard to cut the branch on which he was resting.

If my dear husband Ernest was never there when it counted, it was not through lack of will — except for his desertion in 1914, at which point he left to wind up in the Laurentians. If he was incapable of being present at the birth of our last one, Suzanne, it's for the simple reason that he died before, at age thirty-six. The story of my husband, whose ancestor was a drummer in Wolfe's army, is in no way remarkable and revolutionized nothing either, except for my poor existence. He had various jobs in the same trade — carpenter, house painter, cabinetmaker. He worked for a Jewish storekeeper, not for very long, in a grocery in Côte Saint-Louis. With his thick head of hair, many said he resembled a poet. Certainly not Émile Nelligan. Although my husband was also handsome. More like "the friend of," Arthur de Bussières, also a house painter.

▲▲▲

One evening in March 1928, on payday, Ernest was returning home when a gang of hooligans surrounded him. They wanted his money. They struck him. He told me he defended himself, but, outnumbered, he was defeated in this violent confrontation at the corner of rues Hogan and Ontario. He was found unconscious, lying in a snowbank on an alleyway in the parish. Poorly-treated pneumonia then led to pleurisy and it was all over. On August 28 of the same year, my husband passed away. He left me in mourning with my nine children. As I was saying, nothing remarkable in his anecdotal history: when he was not dead, he was absent and when he was not absent, he was unconscious, left for dead in a snowbank. Which is the same thing: "absent." I lived rough, as they say, I had hard times.

My daughter Suzanne was what today they call a tomboy. Today perhaps they would say she was queer, but I'm not sure. She was born the year of the stock market crash, prelude to the Great Depression. I had to place her in a crèche (the daycares of today) with her younger sisters and her brother Gaston. With Uberte, she grew up in the Sainte-Cunégonde hospice in what is now Little Burgundy. That institution was an orphanage, a crèche, a school, a hospice for destitute old people, all that at once. First in her class, believing she could compensate the emptiness inside her by applying herself to her homework (she was indeed smarter than most), she toed the line in the first years, but quite early on rebelled against religious authority, preferring the mini-wars conducted on the ground to blind obedience to the Grey Nuns.

In terms of education, the nuns were not angels. Driven by a kind of guilty pleasure, they put everything in place to hammer home their principles. They hit hard when they had to correct behaviour deemed deviant. Physically, pinching of the ears was among the most popular ill treatment. Psychologically, group humiliation. Emotions had to first be broken before the group. Making children stand in the corner before the class, they insinuated some not very nice things, totally implausible such as "Would your mother happen to be a woman of easy virtue?" or "Does your mother chase after men?" It's so ridiculous — I who am such a prude, so well behaved, more Catholic than the pope. And so hurtful for my daughter, forced to submit to the humiliations of the Grey Nuns. But I had no choice. My children had to taste that medicine or roam the streets. At least, they would have an education.

Then, from one day to the next, Suzanne radically changed her ways. She traded in her uniform as a boarder — her black serge dress with pleated skirt and the bodice, its stiff white celluloid collar worn with a black bow — for home-made hockey equipment and skates. Imagine two pillows strapped to the shins with old worn-out belts serving as goalie pads: it was hell. When I could finally treat myself to an apartment thanks to the money I'd saved, I immediately repatriated the family. What joy mingled with sadness to finally be able to gather all the kids together beneath one roof! Now living in a huge eight and a half on rue Marie-Anne, corner Mentana, Suzie abandoned good manners for the laws of the street. She swapped her female friends for male friends, did everything to make herself respected, both by her neighbours and by gang members of opposing neighbourhoods. Montreal, in the 1940s, was a powder keg of gangs of wolves.

Speaking of neighbours, there was one called Donalda. Poor thing, she took quite a thrashing. The thrashing of her life. From her balcony on the first floor, the fool had the bad idea of letting an empty bottle of milk drop on my daughter's head. Bottles of milk came in quarts and were made of glass.

At the touch of blood in her sticky mess of hair, she saw red. Suzie planned her little vendetta. Smashing Donalda's face in when the time came was part of her plan A. And a few days later, in an alley, smack, smack! Here, you bitch. *Noli me tangere.* Don't touch me. Isn't that the motto written on the Lippé coat of arms?

▲▲▲

Suzanne had a few fiancés, most of them idlers. Others, of her own admission, were greenhorns who liked to drink. One of her suitors was six foot three and played for the Montreal Royals. My daughter enjoyed free admission at Delorimier Stadium. She could watch all the baseball games. But she set her heart on an Italian, a dashing young man scarcely off the boat. He was hardworking, entrepreneurial, a welder by trade. He worked three shifts a day: eight hours at CN, eight at CP and eight in a small factory in Goose Village, at the foot of the Victoria Bridge. He slept for a few hours in a freight car during his night shift, without the foreman's knowledge.

I remember him as a handyman. If there was a little something to repair on Marie-Anne, Filippo rushed over. The first to help out. He had a good heart. I found him to be good with his hands as well, but as for his mouth, he swore a little too much for my taste, especially when his renovations weren't going smoothly. *Porco Dio, Mannaggia Gesù Cristo, Ma chi t'è morte, Va fan* … I don't understand a damned word of Italian, but I can swear on the head of my mother, Louise Sarrazin, that what he was saying was rather dubious. Suzanne loved him. An Aries. A go-getter. She wanted to build her life with him. Despite my misgivings — it gave my daughter, after the Great Depression, a smaller depression — they were married in Little Italy.

He raised his welding shield and she left her job at *La Presse* to leap into the "Dairy Queen" adventure. An unhoped-for opportunity. Developing a new fast-food chain in Quebec focused on soft ice cream. With my son Gaston and his wife, the first to have gotten wind of this affair, each one signed agreements, deeds to regulate the payment of royalties and organize the opening of the first ventures in Montreal. That was 1956. Imagine. Scarcely three years after landing in Montreal, Filippo, with my daughter, started up two outlets of the new chain. And it worked. The lines were endless. The clientele, on beautiful summer days and, honestly, because they probably had nothing better to do, congregated around the Beaubien outlet, across from the park and at the last minute they had to set up security cordons all around the building to protect the windows. In the late 1950s, Dairy Queen was doing well. Every summer, my daughter Suzie Q and my supposedly atheist son-in-law held down the fort.

▲▲▲

It was there that my adored grandson, Ti-Pouce, was born at 6012 38th Avenue in the Rosemont neighbourhood, where I lived as well, in 1961. Probably he doesn't remember me. He was a year and a half when I died, but that doesn't matter. I saw him grow. His bowling in a league organized by the Bolduc brothers, on Saturday mornings; the baseball games, he was a left-handed pitcher for the Saint-Donat team; later, basketball with the Boucherville Broncos, the jeux du Québec. And I saw him develop, his graduate studies in literature at the Université du Québec à Montreal and later in Rome, his publications, his travels, his highs and his lows. I followed all that from on high, forever absent as I am, forever absent as were his parents, particularly during warm summers, when he was little, busy feeding tongues hanging out in the shape of curly tops. Fortunately there was my eldest, Gaétane, to give a hand with the youngest and in a way play the role of mother, given that Suzanne, meanwhile, had gone from a tomboy to a missing mother, too caught up in her independence — it was the spirit of the times, the years preceding May 68, women's liberation.

Basically, my daughter reproduced with Ti-Pouce and later with Fred the model of the abandoned child, that she herself had endured. It's written in the sound material of the word "sacrifice." In it there is *fils*, meaning son. Why, queen of absences, did I nickname my grandson Ti-Pouce? That comes from vaudeville. You know the couple Eddy Gélinas and Germaine Lippé, Ti-Pit and Fi-Fine? Germaine was my husband's sister. They were in a troupe that toured in the 1940s. They did radio theatre at CKAC. They were popular. Pieces with provocative titles like *Move ton Berlot, Assaye à m'avoir, Ti-Pit prend une bauche*, do you remember? Ti-Pit, Ti-Zoune, Ti-Cune, Tit-Coq, Ti-Clain, why not Ti-Pouce?

Manual of New France

Waves of men casting anchor upon these amaranth shores. Waves without ties, orphans, arriving in disorder, incessant, and bringing everything with them, flesh and fragments from a faraway world, a more unsteady world, different. Crests rise up decisively. Tidal wave of silky pelisses. Men blended with breakers and these crashing down on geographic indentations, immediately giving a name to these anonymous havens. On whom, frankly, should we cast blame? These early arrivals approaching the talk show will see our faces painted in a pumpkin and cranberry colour, then, emulating great white geese, will say, backing up a step, oh my, here are the redskins. Hard to hold it against them. Firebrand illuminating our vast wilderness, doesn't the sun do exactly the same thing when, at dusk, it daubs the face of territories with vibrant makeup?

> *Around my forties I realized I was in a very dark moment in my life. No matter what I did in the "Forest" of reality of 1963 (the year I had reached, absurdly unaware of that exclusion from the life of others that is the repetition of one's own), there was a sense of darkness. I wouldn't say nausea, or anguish: even, in that darkness, to tell the truth, there was something terribly luminous: the light of old truth, if you will, before which there is nothing further to say.*
>
> —Pier Paolo Pasolini, *The Divine Mimesis*, tr. Thomas E. Peterson

From atop this eastern headland made of clear feldspar and granite, we see the West come to meet us. It's an old wampum necklace emerging from the depths of the seas. Yet another scythe tinted gold? As numerous as salmons during the spawning season, men emerged from the shell carved from a nut. Placed immediately in one line, they looked at in the air what they didn't want to see ahead of them.

▲▲▲

At the bottom of a trunk, a tub, they carry the faith and the law of their king. The ocherous sand bears the trace of the foot of an inhabitant of Saint-Malo. Is it that of the leader? This sign left us stunned, or was it stony. The texture of his voice, could it be that it harboured a semblance of Viking? Goatees outline their chins and at the first signal from a bigshot, they charge. On their cloaks smoothed out by the wind, emblems shimmer, leave us perplexed. Aren't these three pine ships moored in the bay over there the bones of the dauphins of the Court of Versailles, beautifully carved by a nautical genius? Is it because of your wide eyes, your beautiful Normandy blue jay eyes that a hand was so kindly held out to you? Didn't you suspect that one day this hand could contain an array of trophies?

Early on we finally understood, at dawn in fact, at the time your long memory arrived on this coast. Didn't we understand that the language barrier, here, would be a futile kind of fortification? Your diplomatic language, mother of the embassy of the seas, reflection of a distinguished logocentric nation that at will can pluck strings, reveal truths, put a damper on things, did we already sense, in our soft chrysalises, that in one breath it would burst open our rivers even better than a gigantic barrel of beer? But on the jagged coast of this *terra nova* where words are a matter of nervous tics, omens can also go mad.

▲▲▲

Decked out in a famous three-cornered hat that we had already eyed, Jacques Cartier reached this country at exactly fifteen thirty-four and pointed out unfavourably the unevenness of the ground with his ringed index finger. At that instant we replied in unison "it's our land." Verbiage! A misunderstanding buried beneath the constant humming of mosquitos! We perceived in your silences set with labradorite, in your secrets tied to our eyes with long braids, even more deposits rumbling and treasures creaking than the Saguenay River is authorized to conceal.

At dawn we finally understand. We needed Jacques Cartier's three-cornered hat at all costs and without delay.

> On this site, it's understood, drive in your cross, but don't dig too deep, you'd touch the root. You've braced sea and world to arrive there. So plant your cross, if that's what you're itching to do, but watch out, don't touch the nerve of this earth. We've seen worse.

But should we still have swapped this three-cornered hat for furs?

▲▲▲

From head to toe you looked us up and down suspiciously. In our clan, did you see even one hunchback? Were you surprised by our bodies, that they could have a head and limbs perfectly connected to a trunk? Did you tremble over so few rumours? Did our polychromatic feathers frighten you so? Unless that was due with our makeshift clothes, our arrows stuck untidily in our daunting quivers.

These vibrating tomahawks oscillating in the gloom, held to our leather straps, the guttural sounds pulled from our throats, do they terrify you? So why did you return crawling to the skeleton of your ships? Why did you decline our hospitality and throw all that nice decorum up in the air? Your crew nodded gently in the harbour on the royal rolling and the pitching was annoying. That night, the sailors slept with one eye open while the other, opened despite the shock, opened on a sagittal plane.

▲▲▲

In a starless sky overlooked by a pale crescent moon, we are those birds that see in the dark, sensing the decoy. And that white crescent, would you have believed, it's the half-moon on Cartier's index finger that was blown up with the blades of an omen, now fastened to the apex, and spies on us. This hooting night from when the harvest is over, our lucifugous tribe, snatched up by the villainous wave, held an unforgettable council at the edge of the woods where no one remained silent or even remained.

Like in autumn flies fall by the ton, your men lose their way. For want of catching fish in the net, or wildfowl returning from the hunt, and no pemmican, you must chew the bark of beech trees and drink Jerusalem artichoke tea. As opposed to bears, you will not get over the winter. Scurvy will figure skate twinned with your organic flora while a new virus has spread behind the groves, inveterate kidnapper, carrying you into the cool humus. Without fresh supplies or a colony, without that insane cycle financed by your capital, you are more destitute than an infantry soldier lost in a wet dream in a snowstorm, than a lead soldier buried in damp sand. Why not lend an ear just once, why not, cast off for good with the crew of angels and the spring thaw?

While we are busily tapping damned loudly but with nimble fingers on our shamanic drums and adjust the volume of tinnitus in the mixed forest,

> you were sleeping stretched out on the ground at the sign of the moon, sleep mangled by the dream of your attacks. You slept, white-eyed.

Sheepish, Donnacona watches two of his sons move away onboard a destroyer before they existed.

Second stage in his promotional tour in North America, Jacques Cartier had to bring back a present to the sovereign so he could remember. After this ravaging, the rats. After the rats, remissness. After that, more raking still.

▲▲▲

The ship disappeared off the rounded coasts.

> When the water wheel made one complete revolution and the albumin of the cosmic egg squirted beyond your floating machines, aboard three canoes repaired with *watap*, a delegation of twenty tawny Mi'kmaq in their tight wolf outfits came to the gangplanks of your ships and presented a premiere of a strange play. Under the authority of an impromptu director, all night we rehearsed the first act of your obscene arrival. If you understand our revolutionary game where the role of prompter is played by the October breeze, thc scenario at most a rustling of leaves, remember that a Greek tragedy fades when the chorus withdraws from the stage. If you seek agreement and harmony among our classical peoples, if you're sensitive to the interferences

> that confused the issue on this sea of errors that led you here, then listen to the promise insinuated in this sad message. Receive as a gift these few pelisses, these moiré skunk furs, and go back from whence you come, we beg you, before the ice buries you.

The arm of the leader, tattooed with confused animals, forms a perfect triangle with his hand shading his eyes. His nerves warmed in a bain-marie. His verve turned over like a glove. He knows that no mirror will send back to him the image of these strange journeys. Scruffy, he returns to his psychic tent. Is that an abyss of flashy memories?

▲▲▲

A colony of maggots will grow in three or four of your quarters of beef and it will not weigh heavily on your scales. A swirl of blue flies will go to land spiritedly on your marrow that they'll suck till there's nothing left, not even the idea of the grotesque. We imagine with some ease these flies during the nice days of the heatwave, stunned by stained glass windows.

They weighed anchor from a faraway port, these club-footed men in shirtsleeves, supposedly come to redeem our souls. Of our redemption, would you still grovel if, in the warmth of evening, in tepees we exchanged our smoke for twilight? A precious wind, carrying pure air, will rise and the chiming of our charms will bury the cheap noise. It will clarify for us that you are springing from an untreatable winter blight and that the two slices of your Greco-Roman brain wage a struggle to death against forgetting. Once, twice, you returned by the same way, but still no communication wire or offspring on the horizon. Bitter fruit of a plundering spring, Domagaya and Taignoagny held circuses in the kingdom of France, commemorated in an artist's book, while here we sobbed their puerile feats, around creeks. Is it such complex gymnastics for men of your kind to keep a vile promise?

▲▲▲

Cut short as they say on your reconnaissance trips that extend from the gulf to the fjord and onto the Île-aux-Oies. Though you may cover all the territory that you like, you'll never extract these gems making your kings dizzy, but rather, these one-legged cyclops, head buried in the solar plexus that contrasts strangely, in welcome, will raise to you a middle finger longer, bonier that an immeasurable stalagmite. Brought back by a tidal wave, you turn around, taking the same sea of errors through which exceptionally you detected us, that is, dreamed us. In reality, you once again half dug us up. What comes next?

Next, nothing else, until the dawns followed one another above our course for another century and then, Lescarbot, De Poutrincourt, the Jesuits and Associates reached the island that they head-on christened Port Royal. The result of what was perhaps a chance incident, the Beothuk tribe disappeared in smoke.

> Also the words ossify around all segments, each of the sentences of this text is based on the critical soundness of an ossuary. A vision of the world in relief, *Weltanschauung* revisited, holophrastic language. When, dancing, the Beothuks make it rain immediately, that's what you call applied semiotics.

We did not want any trouble with the Beothuks. Besides, the new arrivals from an irrevocable loop had tracked them to a magnificent ball of good adventure.

Making history is smoothing the roughness on the surface, it's hoping that the Other will hardly survive the effects of the plane. Didn't they have to raze mountains, knolls, hillocks, raze outgrowths? With the help of the same graphemes located in different places in the word, didn't they have to, sequentially and quickly, prepare the ground for the future passage of the train?

Here begin the story and anecdotes of a people, whose plan stuck in the teeth of a hard of hearing bat fades as the pen of the conquerors uses all the ink in the inkwell.

> The entire pen of history dries up anything in the inkwell. Don't we see couched on paper entire tribes, battered, extravagant stories written in red ink, fastened to a pole? Does indifference stun as much as asking what will people say?
>
> Also they hurried to write at the bottom of the first geographic maps of New France this heartrending legend: "You were here."
>
> Europeans settled comfortably, as far as possible, in a no less wonderful than redundant winter blight.

Grabbed by the collar by a unique lord hooked on latifundium, your good Récollet brothers, their frocks rubbing against their skin, will start in like moths on an old yellowed book, their pious and faithful work of youth. Your fathers with hoods, whose outfits alone snatch mocking smiles from our ghosts, christened in a hurry. Despite the sprays of good faith thrown from atop our improvised graves, their cross did not correctly take hold in that choice of humus. When, in a gushing rapid, they found the turgescent body of Father Viel, his effects and prejudices swallowed up, that was the limit. Your justice raised beneath his long gown had once again, in a horrible grin, revealed his array of bad teeth.

▲▲▲

His name was Samuel de Champlain and he called Quebec this place where the great river is hemmed in by steep banks. In a full field of corn, if not amid the jumble of sunflowers, strawberries and redcurrants, did he sign a jumble of alliances? Certainly. And with the efficiency of a bacterium, the founder walked into our internecine wars to settle there permanently. Assisted by intrepid guides, a few camouflaged big shots, finding a place in a long waterproof rabascaw, he traveled, switching rivers correctly, covered miles and miles like you cover an exquisite corpse with a shroud and, while faultlessly whistling *À la claire fontaine*, he discovered a lake in a slightly pompous way.

▲▲▲

Taking a similar military perspective to the funnel of Quebec City and until its capitulation, an insular people called British temporarily took over the reins. And Quebec City, magically besieged, changed hands like you do with an ecu, a pound sterling or a florin. Yet didn't your kind play in the English Channel where you concealed another map, a secret one? White rabbits, doves come out of a melon hat, Huguenots respecting one another, the two Kirke brothers had us drink a pleasing eau-de-vie, so good it made us forget the lessons of water we learned in life.

> Eau-de-vie, life of water. The bottle emptied of its gin, the invader counted royally on the expected effects. Without harness, Innu and Algonquin invited to speak Franglais. England version 1632 takes over the reins of a mount which in actual fact is without a rider: isn't that the land of no one in particular?

Across from a bottle of gin, we have devoted ourselves to the systematic study of pidgin. Slang to make the Oxford purists blush, to implore Shakespeare to write openly.

How surprised we were, in the early morning, when, hungover, we noticed in the distance a ship flying the French flag.

> Sagard, Brébeuf, Lallemant, Jogues & Associates in procession along the river beneath pitiless baroque clouds. Guarantee of the fathers' success: baptisms at the point of death. Advertising hype. Why this liturgical junk, why all these ballistics? What is the point of giving too much importance to our redemption? With big shovelfuls of earth, myths mingle with the pebbles. There is of course traffic on American souls, traffic jams, scheming, there is of course the start of influence peddling.

And this vessel with its fleur-de-lys mainsail approaching slowly but sharply from the breast-shaped coast, from the aforementioned Tadoussac, in the name of whom? Of Europa.

> On the New Continent isn't it suitable to transplant the Old, for the best? A new Mohawk Jerusalem. At this stage, why not cultivate kaki persimmon, kiwi, learn judo and to play Mikado?

Inside the stone house with rubble foundation, a dwelling adjoining the chapel where two cherubs, in their unisex microfibre Adam costume, act as beams, Champlain, salt and pepper beard, silver head, meditates close to a blue-white flame the three main stages of his settlement plan.

Slouched in his ash wood armchair that dates to before the presence of the emerald ash borer, he hallucinates uplifting harpsichord modulations as an umpteenth steatopygic peasant dies while giving birth in a perhaps uncertain country, but that at least is her own. That was the final vision of the governor before they threw a spray of flowers on his grave. This arable land that he discovered now would cover him in large shovelfuls. But as was its wont, the Court of Versailles was above all that.

▲▲▲

You dreaded they would show up in Quebec City yet your legs trembled at the idea of an assault launched by the hard-headed Iroquois League of Five Nations, in the garden of nothingness, but nevertheless, the humdrum routine was going strong inside fences built with large wooden posts. By candlelight, some resized the map of the New World. Others at dawn packed up their belongings for the long and lucrative beaver trail.

So, right in the middle of a swarming of maggots, at the junction of a utopian desert crossing, you erected another fort on the site where the three rivers flowed together. You drew back from nothing and even less before the West. Were we watching an umpteenth squabble between members of religious orders on the run? At the foot of the hull of vessels in harbour, did you not usurp our vision of the world, so well woven in cross stitch by the words of our language, driving in hollow wood crucifixes that end up spattering our brains? When even our deepest beliefs vanish, the rolling moraine took over, send us even more good indigo waves.

▲▲▲

A melancholy *Wendat* with sagging breasts huddled in a corner of the village of Sainte-Marie, was grinding corn with the butt of an arquebus in a mortar whose concave bottom revealed strange anamorphoses. In the background, her prostrate daughters, palms joined, eyes turned to a lime green sky, in an unwavering harangue, called upon innumerable iguanas and herrings.

> The feathered boaters are trying hard and hum *The river is low-de-vie, This country is low profile*. In the interval, a few succinct conversions in diplomatic language turn the landscape purple. The contact of paddles with the murky film of water enliven the Windigo monster. You want us cannibalistic until transubstantiation "this is my body, this is my blood, drink from it all of you," but you consciously take a stand in a dialogue of the deaf.

Supplanting the brown ones, the black robes advance and hypothetically crackle in the nighttime forest.

> If this tête-à-tête from which we are excluded is only the arena of a combat in which your god and our gods weaken, we ask you if it is the water that bathes eternity or eternity that shines at the end of our blood?

These dark robes have come to stealthily exorcise us, but why do those who don them drive back the crows from tree to tree? Did we think we were losing our way or the mistral at the bottom our London bottles? At dawn we regain consciousness, it was to smoke, it was to carry out unusual rituals at the spellbinding sound of spoon playing.

▲▲▲

Visibly overcome by a rather vile nightmare, the shaman who often wanders claims to us he made a swap with the Old World, exchanging his moose antlers and shimmering cape for a bow tie, a Bavarian top hat, a tuxedo, imported from cities, items that he now sports idiotically. Beside himself, did he not predict that an ephemeral dew of insecticide was deposited, one fine October morning, on the valleys of Amerindia?

▲▲▲

False peace signed with a cross on a ground carpeted in couch grass. Below on the right a document blown away in smoke. In the background, a magenta twilight and Iroquois crouching, the cannons of their muskets enthusiastically polished. Just as the trees conceal the forest, spiked as they are by magnetic forces, so the clichés of a war of prosecution, without artifice but sadly three-dimensional, escape being brought to light through an open wound on the body of a scout. Crazy allies, we walk under cover of darkness, death dangling at our sides. No religion, no munition. No money no candy at the metropolitan candy shop. Is it possible that we are but at the mercy of the foliage and the wind? And when we die, will it at least be with healthy teeth?

Trappers before fur quotas were established, trappers merrily left to wander in the heart of the hairiest forest, if not at the heart of its added value. Harbingers of a trade fundamentally rigged. So much traffic in the woods requires that at least animism lead. All these Canucks fascinated by the border, magnetized by the Rockies like magnets on a fridge, jump, each more than the other, over the memorial fences beneath the infinitely fierce gaze of deer whose contorted snouts betray disdain. Must we absolutely handle these Canucks on snowshoes with white gloves, they for whom the country is a basic racket, an open bar, if not an unmarried mother who has left for good? Is it Pan playing the reed pipe that we are hearing there? Is it the ones we called the renegades? These renegades cheerfully break the universalist laws of the clan. They feast on corn among the ferruginous geese, daubing their bodies with paint like warriors, and to top it off, in a revival of lustful activity, marry the most beautiful of our squaws that they smash in the end for full tubs of raspberries. Give Étienne Brûlé the finger and Radisson the coureur de bois can go screw himself.

▲▲▲

Beneath their black robes, good sisters cultivate many varieties of mushrooms. At the same time haven't they foreseen *ante litteram* the invention of penicillin? Instilling the not absolute idea that a convent can be just, wasn't that the *modus operandi* for the jumbled recruitment of our virgins? A jail is worth a patch of fog in the minds of these girls. While with a great many handsaws the religious boarding school was erected on a hill, from these despised chairs emerge the sweet smells of absenteeism. Did you dream of a new Jerusalem? Here it is, planted deep in the boreal forest. Inventing that, you hid your eyes, for our family structures verged on that of a harem. May this thorn filed away in our hearts one day shine forth from the bottom of your drawer!

> Good gentle sisters, who in your mental cupboards put away the games of hopscotch, jump ropes, rag dolls. A skull lying on the table next to the letter being written, with the inkwell, the seal, the office illuminated by candlelight, act as memento mori.

The temporary stockades encircling your town carve a jagged horizon. Do these signs let us believe that your colony is being built, is progressing? Most certainly. With evidence to prove it, this concrete statement that the accumulated layers of sawdust draw everywhere blond snow drifts in the heart of the summer months. We see your boys and girls at dusk, when it's time to open the kegs, going to pick strawberries in the patch. Do you see ours? No. It's status quo, they stay in place between maple and catechism.

▲▲▲

The threat of a chic Iroquoia hovered smoothly, when, filled with daring, he landed in Ville-Marie. An early hospital, a town plan and fortifications quickly erected gave the site the look of self-sufficiency. Would the Iroquois returning to the island be what they are without being tightly tied to the Anglos? Of Osheaga, there remains only a right of way. Were you trying to interpret beyond Mount Royal the carbonic code of a smoke so opaque that came to this statement of the obvious: the enemy saw red. In Ville-Marie criss-crossed with hope and daisies, perhaps a hub for furs, a window that one day stretched to Albany and even Manhattan, you didn't dare imagine, gently snuggling in your gleaming fortifications, how long the days can be after the Assumption and the vertical abduction of a woman. Ave Maria and Ville-Marie.

That evening the air was at its loveliest in honour of an umpteenth fair to which we are all invited. For the fur trade market, you hoped to see strut in single file our bodies daubed with malachite-coloured paint, our eyes made up with kohl. On the other hand, we came down all together from the Huron country with soft pelisses dangling from our shoulders. Do you take the bartering by the horns, and do we take your knick-knacks for hard cash? Your counters stink of alcohol, it doesn't matter, we have a good laugh when we invite ourselves into your circle. The return trip would seem even longer without your escort. Games of skill and outlandish never-ending official talk. The origin of pilosity long reviewed by interpreters who are underpaid under the table.

▲▲▲

We sensed it, you'd be inclined to lynch that drunken Wendat girl who dances tightly, spasmodically behind cool groves for the excited blue eye of the thirty-fifth infantry regiment. What is that roar? A fighter of anachronic air forces flying at low altitude, an ear-splitting noise.

Imminent confrontation, the theatre played out on our bruised land.

> You are hungry and imagine on silver platters served without too much care a Huron head from which was conserved the black tuft in the middle of the skull.

The Iroquois tribe tried to appease its irritation by dancing on the triumphal cove. Our scouts lying in ambush need only read some sign in the swaying wampum to discover the hour and place of the fratricidal assault, but will they have the time to see the moon unroll its morbid reflections and fluorescent green on the Mohawk village before a hail of arrows skewers them.

> Naïve and cheerful and enveloped in a cloud of sea spray on the pearly shores of Lake Simcoe turning pink in the twilight, the Wendats of Ossossané also had to endure their visit. What could your robes, sepia at first, ebony afterwards, hope from them in return for a slim bar of St. Catherine's taffy?

Through a veinlet where the night bursts in, they pounce on our scenario. Alongside a malarial cesspool a panoply of various species of insects teams up, and their leader, this old lover of the Atlantic coasts, hugs against his chest a prisoner with whom he really wanted to unite.

▲▲▲

Forerunners of the punk movement, semi-nomadic with spiked hair, holding clubs of a rather bruised mauve. A night without hooting of the moon, when the air whispered electric groans, the enemy swooped down on the dully asleep town. Semi-nomadic with half their heads shaved, a deposit of slate, of chalk, left in the back of their gaze, faces stained with the rust from old trade axes. Semi-nomadic with British arquebuses, cannons polished with the venom of asps. Bends in clear streams are jumping with as many showy troops and soon will tear us to shreds. Semi-nomadic with bodies covered in a medley of covers, moccasins with seams coming undone run in every direction among the longhouses that won't last long. Are the heads of Hurons served with offal? Hearts and scalps brandished high on the strand of Lake Simcoe.

Iroquois, atypical, prototypical enemy, concept and plan sketched in red pencil. Manufactured, screwed on, fastened piece by piece on the assembly line, from fenders to the horn, from the electronic sensor to the transmission belt. The model broken in, painted, verified before being released. Camouflage the series number, that tiny yellow mark etched on the lower back. We have difficulty seeing what will happen at the end of the chain. Iroquois, poor imaginary enemy, both bolt and monkey wrench, plastic mould and big Corvette. A convertible vehicle to arrive at its ends. Buick Machiavelli. Ford Teleonomy. Mustang razzia. Finally reaching Detroit where Cadillac landed.

▲▲▲

There can be found a considerable heap of smoking bodies in the early morning. Scattered torsos, heads like stalks of cabbage or similar, pushed by a macabre wind, were still rolling when we arrived on the crimson carpet.

Unfortunate fate waved a white flag and all that remained of Huronia were a few eels drying on the Adirondack curves of canoes. Would you like to change the ocean into wine? It's done. It's vermillion.

A cloud of brownish cherubs, neophytes, were rummaging in the miscible ectoplasm, of Canadian martyrs, hesitating between two elements, heart or soul, wondering which they should first eat, but on closer examination, it was a pack of famished coyotes licking life after death.

A fissure was running through the Huron community, making the village of the dead sway on its axis and

while your skin tanned at the height of the heatwave,
some of your heads would likely fall.

We were cannon flesh, while we canonized them. Huronia: was it a bad dream become mass grave that an exasperating dawn illuminated despite itself?

▲▲▲

The man who saw the man who saw the bear is, to put it briefly, a wolf for man. Yet, having slid in their uniforms accompanied with gleaming medals, with golden stripes, Wolfe and Montcalm pad along from the sheep pen to the battlefield. On the high chessboard that is the Plains of Abraham, troops from both camps, with the taste of failure in their mouths, without losing their calm, get down to serious work. Is it that? One knee on the ground, in firing position, the noose is tightening, the soldiers of the infantry fall, drums beating, spirals that form on the grass as many fruit peels, the majority apples. The end of a battle in record time, can we still call that an end? Can we still call that a battle? The French land forces still don't possess the technique of clever ambush and razzia as cannonballs still fly over our oblate nightmares. Are you still impervious to our strategies? Why did you fight in open country?

North American Retrospective

When someone leans over me, overturned like a ladybug, on my back, and asks me my age, intuitively I open my right hand, my golden elytra, deploy the pentadactyl part of my body that has vanished in ancient times. I am the age of my hand, I tell, the age of a hand span. From this almost fetal position, I can see perfectly the curve of the Earth and the continent. Am I prisoner of a cage of flesh? Enveloped in stardust? Fully stretched out and flanked by a figurine of a polar bear, I contemplate a sky, if it's not the cover of a tomb, where painted in fresco is a dinosaur-bird and moons cleverly traced on boreal suns. And I dream of flying away.

We stood on the road and looked at his back.
One could see very far in the cold air. I was five years old.
—Heiner Muller, *The Father*, tr. Carl Weber

The other day my father said, filled with good intentions, "Tomorrow we leave for Acapulco." Fallen from a chair made of braided corn leaves, my mother could not believe her ears. "Apparently," he continued in a light tone, "Acapulco is a fashionable destination. So shall we be fashionable and go?" Apparently one week on the road in the Plymouth is enough or with a hundred thousand flaps of a monarch butterfly's wings you can, once metamorphosized, land in Mexico City. I fell back to sleep on these thoughts, small onyx stone that I am, slowly sinking straight to the bottom in a river thousands of years old. Suddenly my mother lowered her face to me. Through the water depth, it seemed to me as undulating as it was pentagonal. Although it was early, I noted that my mother's face was covered with make-up, powder, rouge, and her mascara-coated eyelashes — it was as if she were made up for a ceremony, prepared for a long journey.

"Get up, my Ti-Pouce!" They've been calling me that for several generations, might as well say always. Is it you who's come to say hello, Mom? Is it you decked out in your finest snake-*coatl* dress? Is it you approaching, aboard a canoe, as if bewitched? My child's body in its cage-sarcophagus gave a start, but I regained my composure as I identified the sweet painted face.

My bedroom, really, is a ceiling, four plasterboard walls, white screens where a shadow puppet show is performed. Outside it's a particularly cold December day and inside it's Sunday, might as well say eternity. At the window, frost and wind are visible for some.

▲▲▲

Under the widening beam of the kitsch orange torchière lamp in the living room, I see my father bent over the road map, highlighting in red the journey from Montreal to Acapulco. Seen from here, America seems to me immense and fabulous and above all a large organic body. I see a quantity of small vessels, capillaries, intersecting to infinity. Yet it's only an unfolded rectangle of paper placed on the table. With the hoarse voice of a hungry lion, my father analyzed. "At all costs, tomorrow we must go beyond the Toronto Tartar," — that's his expression — some sort of Rubicon, I surprised myself as a budding historian — "before noon." I remember perfectly the electricity that was in the air and also the anxiety, the unknown, the emotions that large spaces free up when we approach them, while they, the large spaces, at the same time, recede.

The 1961 Plymouth with the two long salmon-coloured spoilers parked on snowy rue Duquesne, located at the edge of Notre-Dame-des-Victoires in the east of the city, a street swept by drifting wind, it's my father's Plymouth (two spoilers that make you think of the runners of a sled) and it waits in a black cloud for us to place our luggage in it — four canvas travel bags, on one of which was sewn the Dairy Queen logo with the soft ice cream cone and its curly top.

> Time distorts facts relentlessly. It was really a 1962 Cadillac Sedan de Ville, black with white wall tires. I have the proof here. In these black-and-white photos, my father, sporting his sunglasses, poses proudly in front of his black Cadillac and by his side his three-year-old son, both outlined in exotic settings such as Miami's South Beach, Fort Lauderdale, Ciudad de México, etc.

Are departures only exciting for three-year old kids? I doubt it. One thing is certain: the jubilation reached its height at the corner of Bellechasse and Christophe-Colomb as I saw through the oval that my warm fingers drew in the fogged window an overturned Volkswagen Beetle, whose wheels, whatever they say, are still turning. The image of this little ladybug's wheels turning in mid-air — a combination of a road accident and synchronicity — followed me at least to Fort Wayne, Indiana.

Philosophizing at the wheel, my father called out: "If God is the wheel, man is the puck."

> I think he meant "puppet." My father, a descendant of the Samnites, a people that dominated by force the region of Campania at the time of the Roman

Empire, often distorts words. Instead of "sleep" he says "seep." A "crocodile" becomes "coccodrile" and *échelle*, the French word for ladder," extraordinarily becomes "Shell," the service station.

Not showing any indication of idleness, signs of service stations slip past one after the other at one o'clock in the morning when everyone is usually sleeping. The Texaco banner is succeeded by Gulf, BPs, Shell, in fact, Esso, Champlain, all the dispensaries pallidly lit by dull fluorescents. And each time that on Earth the lights of a service station go dark at night, a new star is born in the universe, in another galaxy.

▲▲▲

Lying curled up on the back seat of the Plymouth, beneath my multi-coloured striped Hudson's Bay blanket, at noon, I open my eyes, apparently in Toronto. The cracks coldly etched into the black and white leatherette seat carry me far away from myself.

World: Be, and be good;
exist nicely, do that, try to, aim at, tell me all [...]
—Andrea Zanzotto, "To the World," *The Selected Poetry and Prose of Andrea Zanzotto*, tr. Patrick Barron

In the front, my mother was a perfect co-pilot.

Patting her mouth with her hand, making it seem she could have issued a Native American war cry when she was simply yawning, my mother says: "Where does all this insistence to reach the South come from, like a drop of sweat?" But the gusts of wind and blizzards held the answer in their own way.

The figurehead that any crew deserves, this profile of a loving mother with her distant Abenaki roots facing southwest, the map of the United States skillfully folded on her knees.

Saving space in the Plymouth. Is that to say "ergonomics" before the era of ergonomists? Crows hopping on the shoulder of the highway system or set out in rows on electrical or telephone wires, hard to say, call to mind an abacus. Flying on the x-axis toward the horizon. Crossing the northern belt of Detroit, that my mother, with a strong French accent, calls the thruway, I see from the elevation Afro-Americans lighting camp fires here and there and, across from the glow lighting their faces, they are doubled with laughter in the twilight.

Hot coffee poured into the thermos, then drive along, watch again the white wall tires, invent, write and even become the road in a landscape of ink. The American highways have in common that they are all bordered by green coats of arms.

> I am afraid that the road will be long, not too, longer than the day in any case, that the sun will tow it. That was true until they held us at the border like a sphincter, if not like a Sphinx on the fringes of Thebes, in the desert.

I discovered this lucky charm. A stuffed baby crocodile, lying near the rear window of the Plymouth. I nibble on its paws, I like the taste of wet ash in my mouth. Fossilized index finger. I start on the tail, until when and under what latitude will this living fossil preserved by taxidermy hold up? Till Wyandotte, Michigan.

> Cars parked at the foot of snowbanks in the motel lot. A light that slows down the eye's progress. The night

> is a tin can resisting a can opener that turns and turns and turns, relentlessly.

I think I am in love with a fair-haired girl, the one who's turning around on the billboards, the bottles of Coppertone, in my head, everywhere.

> The black poodle pulling on the bathing suit to remove it from the little girl, on the brown plastic bottle, is always me.

Terre Haute, Pocahontas, Seneca, Toledo, St. Clair, Muskogee, Lebanon, Rolla, Sapulpa, Bristow, Chandler, Prague, Whitesboro, Bourbon, St. Robert, Kankakee, Champaign, Mattoon, Carbondale-Marion, Forrest City, Little Rock, Prescott, Sulphur Springs, Waco, Temple City. All these backwaters through which I pass.

But it's in the heart of Oklahoma that the mass with two drive wheels turns off, heading south for good. Two-headed eagle with bronze wings swooping down on its prey. The tip of a pickaxe forcing the matter to split. A drill turning in the woods. TNT in the hollow of a mountain.

Each grain of sand in the overturned hourglass that slips through the bottleneck is a wheel and in the egg-shaped lower vessel begins to pile up like a car cemetery. Could it be that time no longer moves?

> To mark out the time again on this half-Laurentian, half-Gondwanan continent, one by one I patiently fit in all the pieces of the child's puzzle, a fragile but formative construction jiggling on my thighs.

Telephone poles pattern the landscape. But are they really telephone poles? Is there anyone? Is literature communication? My eyes follow the imaginary line that runs dancing on the window and splits the universe in two.

> The planet, the continent, the country, the plain, and somewhere a grain of sand rolls so slowly on the road that the Sprit of the places overlooking us suddenly fall asleep, the book slips, which falls, falls, keeps on falling.

My heart is heavy, tightly packed like these poles. I miss opportunities to wave to these young people, highway markers in a small parking lot and my mother assures me that these people are indeed hitchhikers.

At eye-level, close to Dallas on the 35, I alone happen to read a word. A first: "Motel." I isolate the five incandescent letters against the backdrop of an inn, dissect them. It is a word twinkling fully at nightfall — layering it, superimposed. Implosion of joy, exhilaration of discovery.

I entered into the magical, sacrificial, sequential world of letters. The pistons in an engine block. Then after a few hours, I manage to differentiate "Hotel" from "Motel." Is that a question of blown glass, of aeration, of neon tubes, slanting more or less, placed across the world? Read: is this reaching new ranges of meaning, running alongside them, rushing to the sea with such or such a word in such or such water? In reality, I am only beginning to give equal attention to words and to the world.

Winter broken in two on the knee goes crack! And the shards of glass end up flying on the prickly curves of cacti. All points of the compass abolished, wiped out in keeping to the wandering of the road. While the dawn jumps up, does the border rise to the surface?

▲▲▲

Mental fence, sharing of land between Laredo and Nuevo Laredo.

> Once the southern border of the United States has been crossed, there is a Mexico in layers and a Mexico in levels. I nibble harder at my favourite crocodile — an eagle in full flight transforms into a little archaeopteryx, its pupil is a meteorite, inside the global and the invisible are concentrated.

Mexico, the sound of which my puerile lips endorse, is handsome. Well broken in by the road it took and recreated, the Plymouth system, which makes heads wearing sombreros turn at the mere sight of its spoilers, and which in fact is a dinosaur-bird flying low in a deserted landscape, drives along at breakneck speed, all ready to attack the high plateaus of the Sierra Madre.

Ahead, the road. Behind, nothing. Does a chasm open at the place where pebbles hurtling down widen the abyss? I rely on my father's composure. At this altitude, the asphalt drinks, smokes. Gods leaning on the counter of Death.

The spirit of arid lands returns to watch the Plymouth pass with its white side tires.

So many mountains and a road link without a guard rail. The light-coloured skulls depicted on the asphalt hide the breathing, the slightest gestures, the least outlined plans.

Monterrey located at the foot of the elevation: was that just the announcement of a point toward which we climbed, already buried, when the mountain formed a chain where punishment occurred?

Men, women, children of the village ran toward the Plymouth system, gathered there.

> Car-horse-carcass. A royal bird of prey lands on it, tears off another metal strip. I search for a place on the back seat where I can lie low, in vain.

We lay ourselves open to the world, the world lays itself open to us so that we tumble down it. We, the Rastas, the gringos, the Tabarnacos in their sarcophagus, that the villagers watch pass. I see us and all these people with a child's eyes. Time is on my side, I gather air in my lungs. They see me grow larger through the prism of a bottle of Coke.

Acknowledgements

My thanks go to my family, immediate and extended, without whom the writing of *L'Origine du futur* would have been unlikely. Thanks are owed to my ancestor, Ernest, on my mother's side, for beginning that adventure on Canadian soil during the Battle of the Plains of Abraham, and to my father, Filippo, for beginning his own, when he left his native Campania in 1953. Thanks to my paternal grandfather Giovanni and my maternal grandmother Geneviève for telling the anecdotal history of our presence in North America, because they were here before I was. Thank you to my son Émilien and my wife Antonella for their closeness as I pursued this timeless, never-ending adventure. Thanks are also owed to Lucie Lippé and Pierre Beaudin for their patient research as the Lippé family genealogists. I am especially grateful to Gilles Thérien, director of the university research group "L'Indien imaginaire" (The Imaginary Indian) of which I was a part at Université du Québec à Montréal some forty years ago. Thanks to him, I was able to open myself up to First Nations people and become inspired by history, told as a backdrop to this book. I also wish to thank my publishers at Éditions Mains libres, Stéphane Despatie and Corinne Chevarier, for their careful and impassioned reading, which certainly had an impact on the final version of *L'origine du future*, as well as Michael Mirolla and Connie Guzzo-McParland of Guernica Editions for the confidence they placed in the new life of this text, commissioning, thanks to the Canada Council for the Arts, its passage into English carried out by Jonathan Kaplansky, to whom I am especially grateful for his exceptional translation and his generosity of spirit.

About The Author

A novelist (*On achève parfois ses romans en Italie*) and short-story writer (*Qu'il fasse ce temps*), **Francis Catalano** has also published eight collections of poetry. Born in Montreal in 1961, he has translated texts by several contemporary Italian poets and novelists, including Pier Vittorio Tondelli, Edoardo Sanguineti, Antonio Porta and Mario Luzi. For his work on Valerio Magrelli's *Instructions pour la lecture d'un journal*, the Literary Translators' Association of Canada awarded him the John Glassco Prize. Some of his books have been translated into Italian, Spanish and English; a selection of his poems, entitled *Where Spaces Glow* and translated by Christine Tipper, was published at Guernica Editions. He was also shortlisted for the Governor General's Literary Award for poetry for *Qu'une lueur des lieux*, a collection for which he was awarded Grand Prix Québecor at the 26th Trois-Rivières International Poetry Festival.

About the Translator

Jonathan Kaplansky is a literary translator of French in Montreal and won a French Voices Award to translate Nobel Prize winner Annie Ernaux's *Things Seen (La vie extérieure).* He has also translated many well-known Québec authors including Jonathan Bécotte, Hélène Dorion, Lise Gauvin, Louis-Philippe Hébert, Hélène Rioux and Lise Tremblay. He has twice sat on the jury for the English-translation category of the Governor General's Literary Awards and three times on the jury for the John Glassco Prize, which he chaired in 2022. He recently translated *Not Even the Sound of a River* by Hélène Dorion and *Like a Hurricane* by Jonathan Bécotte; the translation was shortlisted for the David Booth Award.

Printed by Imprimerie Gauvin
Gatineau, Québec